Christmas
with the Neighbours

PATRINA McKENNA

Publisher: Patrina McKenna

patrina.mckenna@outlook.com

ISBN-13: 978-0-9932624-9-4

Also by Patrina McKenna

Romantic comedy with a twist!

Truelove Hills
Truelove Hills – Mystery at Pebble Cove
Truelove Hills – The Matchmaker
Granny Prue's Bucket List
Christmas with the Neighbours

Feel good fantasy for all the family!

GIANT Gemstones
A Galaxy of Gemstones
The Gemstone Dynasty
Enrico's Journey
Summer Camp at Tadgers Blaney Manor

DEDICATION

For my family and friends

MEET THE NEIGHBOURS

THE LACEY'S
Carol, Don, and Justin

The Lacey's have lived at No. 10 Nasturtium Close, in Milford-le-Mont, for twenty-nine years. Their twenty-eight-year-old son, Justin, now lives in Scotland with his girlfriend, Rachel.

For the last three Christmases, Justin and Rachel have gone skiing to Vermont – leaving Carol and Don home alone. Carol is determined that this year will be different, and she acts on impulse when she sees an advertisement for a lakeside lodge that's available over the holiday period.

THE PRITCHARD'S
Dora, Jez, and Amy

The Pritchard's moved into No. 9 Nasturtium Close, two weeks after the Lacey's moved into No. 10.

Dora and Carol were both pregnant at the time. The Pritchard's daughter, Amy, was born four weeks before Justin. Amy still lives in Milford-le-Mont. She's a teacher at the village primary school and has her own apartment.

Dora and Jez Pritchard are best friends with Carol and Don Lacey.

THE CASSIDY'S

Sharon, Ryan, Jack, and Lottie

The Cassidy's are the newest neighbours in Nasturtium Close. They moved into No. 18, over the road from the Lacey's, six months ago. Jack is six and Lottie's three.

When Sharon heard that the Lacey's and Pritchard's were heading five hours north to Little Marchampton, for a fortnight break away, she was keen to join them. With all the renovation work the Cassidy's are undertaking, they are relieved to be going away over Christmas and New Year.

THE APPLEBY'S

Edna and Bill

The Appleby's live next door to the Lacey's at No. 11 and have resided in Nasturtium Close for over fifty years. Bill loves his garden and is friendly with the neighbours. Edna is a private person and takes to her bed when she's having one of her "bad days". No-one really knows Edna.

It, therefore, came as somewhat of a shock to the neighbours when Edna and Bill invited themselves along for the Christmas holidays. Edna put it down to one of her "funny feelings". Bill was just happy to go with the flow; in fact, he was quite excited about going on holiday with the neighbours. Unlike his wife, Bill was popular in Nasturtium Close.

1

THE HOLIDAY SEASON

Carol Lacey ran into the back garden and headed straight for her husband Don's man shed. 'I've just had the most dreadful news. Rachel's dumped Justin, and he's on his way home for Christmas.'

Don placed the model boat he'd been working on for the past week onto his workbench. 'I never liked Rachel. I view it as good news.'

Carol tugged at her hair as she paced around the shed. 'I didn't like her either; it's Christmas I'm worried about. What are we going to do about Justin? We're going away with the neighbours on Saturday, and the lodge is fully booked. Justin was supposed to be going to Vermont with Rachel. Well, there's nothing else for it – we won't be able to go.'

Mrs Appleby poked her head over the fence. 'Everything all right over there, Carol?'

Don raised a bushy eyebrow and peered over his glasses. 'Well, I'm still going to the lodge. Bill's relying on me to bring the Christmas cheer. He needs a bit of that after spending the whole year alone with her next door.'

Carol hissed. 'Don't you go talking about Edna Appleby like that. It's important we get along with the neighbours, she's not as bad as everyone thinks.'

'Well, I hope you're right. It was your idea in the first place that we all went away together.'

'I thought we were going to be on our own again this Christmas. I didn't want the two of us rattling around the house like a couple of spare parts. I knew the Pritchard's next door would be up for it, and I'm thrilled the Cassidy's are joining us with their two young children. I just didn't expect the Appleby's to invite themselves along.'

Don waved to Edna Appleby through the shed window, and she jumped off the plastic step she kept next to the fence for when she heard Carol in the garden. Carol Lacey was a lovely woman; her husband freaked Edna out, though. Don was always calm and steady, with a ready smile and a wave. Apart from that, Edna didn't have much to do with him. It was as if he could see straight through her – maybe he knew her secret. She hadn't told Bill; how could Don have found out?

Don picked up the model boat again and scrutinized it through a magnifying glass. 'I think we're overlooking the obvious, Carol. Amy Pritchard was always keen on Justin. Jez and Dora will be delighted if he joins us for the holidays; they were worried about Amy being a bit left out.'

'But where will he sleep?'

'The sofa. I'm sure he slept on a few sofa's when he was at university. He's a strapping twenty-eight-year-old now. A fortnight on a sofa won't phase him.'

Carol sighed. 'I do hope you're right, Don.'

'Do you mean about Amy having a soft spot for Justin, or Justin accepting the fact that he'll be sleeping on the sofa?'

'Both! I'd love Amy as a daughter-in-law. The Pritchard's are like family already. Remember all the times we couldn't get Justin and Amy out of the treehouse? They used to be the best of friends. Now that Rachel's off the scene, I have high hopes for those two. Why are you always so clever, Mr Lacey?'

'Just call it instinct, my dear. I was born with it.'

*

On Saturday, Justin dragged his case into the hallway

of the lodge. 'Which room's mine, Mum?'

Don put his arm around his son. 'Remember the saying "last one in"?'

Justin nodded. 'First one out.'

Don laughed. 'No! You remember. The last one in for dinner on a Sunday had to sit in-between Granny and Gramps. Your cousins always rushed to the table first, but you made sure you were last one in so that Granny would pile your plate high with extra roast potatoes and Yorkshire puddings.'

'And, Gramps always said it was "good to be last as there were always benefits".'

'Exactly!' Don pointed to the sofa. 'There's your bed. The benefit of being the "last one in" this time means that you can watch TV into the early hours if you keep the sound down. You can raid the fridge in the middle of the night with no-one hearing you sneaking down the stairs, and you don't have to make your bed. Just leave your bedclothes to one side, and your mum will sort them out. I might even join you in an armchair if your mum's snoring gets out of hand after a few too many snowballs – she loves those with a couple of cherries on a cocktail stick at Christmas.'

'You could have told me before we set off on a five-hour drive. I'm not sleeping on a sofa for a fortnight.'

The lodge door flew open, and Amy breezed in.

'Justin! I haven't seen you for years. How are things? Mum tells me you're being very manly and sleeping on the sofa for the holidays. Come here and give me a hug, we've got so much catching up to do.'

Don held the front door open for Amy's parents – Dora and Jez Pritchard – who were heavily laden with luggage. 'Glad you made it safely. We've only just arrived too.'

Edna and Bill Appleby appeared on the landing. Bill smiled down at his neighbours. 'We made it in good time. We've chosen a room up here with an en-suite and balcony. It's very nice, isn't it, Edna?'

Edna grinned and looked down at the stunned faces from her superior position. Mission accomplished. The early bird gets the worm and on this occasion, she had chosen the best room for the Appleby's.

Dora smiled at Carol. 'Thank you so much for making all the arrangements. Do you know which rooms are ours?'

Carol suppressed her annoyance. She was going to suggest that Edna and Bill had the best room – she didn't expect them to just grab it for themselves. Not very neighbourly and quite underhand sprang to mind. 'Well, there's a double and single downstairs with a bathroom. Would you be happy to take those with Amy? One of the rooms upstairs has bunk beds so I thought the Cassidy's should all stay up there together.'

Jez pulled two cases towards the downstairs bedrooms. 'These will suit us fine, Carol. You've been a star sorting this out for us all. These things don't happen without people like you around.'

Amy bounced up and down on the sofa. 'I hope my bed's as comfortable as this. I think you've done all right here, Justin. You were never one to go to bed early from what I remember. You'll be able to watch TV in front of an open fire all night if you want.'

Once inside her bedroom, Amy flopped onto her bed. She didn't want to be here for the holidays, and now her parents had given her the responsibility of making sure Justin had a good time. Life was not fair.

After unpacking, Dora headed for the kitchen to find Carol stocking the cupboards with a food delivery they had ordered from the local shop. 'That's good service. They said after four, and it's only five past now. Any news of the Cassidy's?'

Carol nodded towards the window. 'I've just seen their car pull up outside.' Carol shouted to her son, 'Justin! The Cassidy's have arrived. They're such a nice family. You'll love their children, Jack's six and little Lottie's three.' Justin switched to the sports channel on the TV and pulled the footstool closer before putting his feet up.

Don and Jez went outside to help Sharon and Ryan Cassidy with their luggage. Sharon made Jack hold hands with Lottie. 'Now go inside you two. Don't let go of her Jack; you know how fast she is. Make sure you watch her with the stairs.'

Jack walked into the lodge, holding onto his sister. As soon as his mother was out of sight, he let go of Lottie's hand and jumped onto the sofa next to an alarmed Justin. 'Can we watch Spiderman?'

Abandoned Lottie burst out crying, and Dora went over to pick her up. 'There, there. You know everyone here, Lottie, apart from Justin. Let's go and meet him. He used to be little like you once, now he's all grown up.'

Lottie noticed the plate of biscuits on the coffee table, and she stopped crying. Dora wedged the young girl on the sofa between Justin and Jack. 'You wouldn't mind keeping an eye on the children, would you Justin? It's just while Sharon and Ryan take their bags upstairs.'

A windswept Sharon struggled into the lounge armed with toys. She was relieved to see her children sitting quietly on the sofa watching children's TV. 'Hi, I'm Sharon. You must be Justin. A live-in childminder is the answer to our prayers.' Sharon looked over her shoulder. 'Ryan! Come and meet Justin, he's great with the children.'

After letting Jack and Lottie eat as many biscuits as they liked, Justin was in demand. Lottie followed him around everywhere, and Jack was keen to have a playmate. They were engrossed in a game of snakes and ladders when Ryan came down the stairs. 'All unpacked! Come upstairs, you two, there's a surprise in your bedroom.'

Lottie and Jack dragged an unwilling Justin upstairs too. When Ryan opened the door to their bedroom, the children squealed with delight at the sight of bunk beds. Ryan held onto the ladder as Jack climbed safely to the top.

Ryan winked at Justin. 'Don't worry, mate. Sharon was only joking about you being our resident childminder; once the kids are in bed, I'll buy you a pint. There's a pub down the road next to a Chinese takeaway. How about we offer to collect dinner tonight and pop next door for a swift one on the way?'

Justin winked at Ryan and shook his hand. The Christmas holidays with the neighbours had begun, and Justin was surprised to find himself smiling. Maybe the next two weeks wouldn't be such a chore after all.

2

CATCH-UP

The following morning Carol suggested Justin and Amy took a walk into the village. Justin noticed Amy's mood drop as soon as they left the lodge. She wasn't keen to talk about herself, and she was uncharacteristically remote. On top of that, it was far too cold to be roaming the lanes of Little Marchampton in the far north of England a week before Christmas with no hat or gloves.

Amy noticed Justin shiver and thrust his hands deep into his jacket pockets. 'You're not going to last a fortnight up here without better clothing. I thought you were going to Vermont for Christmas? Didn't you think of bringing your thermals, or at least a scarf?'

'I left in a rush. Besides, it never snows in England at Christmas. I can't remember a white Christmas back home. That's why Rachel was so keen to go away the last three years. There's something magical about snow at this time of the year.'

Amy tutted. 'You're just stupid, Justin. I bet Rachel booked the holidays and did all your packing didn't she?' Justin nodded. 'Well, you're on your own now, and you'd better get real. It can get cold in this country over Christmas and New Year. Whether you like it or not, we're both stuck here until the 2nd of January and, trust me, snow is forecast over the next few days.'

Justin's teeth chattered. 'Snow, really?'

'Yes, snow. I hope you've got your credit card on you; we need to get you kitted out.' Amy pushed Justin inside a men's clothing shop, where she slumped into a chair while he chose some practical clothes.

Leaving the shop, armed with carrier bags, Justin's mood began to lift. 'You've always told me straight, Amy. I like that about you. I'll buy you a hot chocolate in the café over the road, and you can tell me what you've been up to since I left for university.'

Amy warmed her hands on the steaming mug. 'You go first, why did Rachel dump you? She was your longest relationship, wasn't she? It must have been three years.'

'She dumped me because she thought I was

cheating on her. It's no big deal.'

'Were you cheating on her?'

'No. It's a long story, one I would prefer to put behind me. What's going on with you? You were happy when we were in the lodge, but as soon as we walked down the drive, your mood changed.'

'I've just got a lot on my mind with work at the moment. I don't want to bother my parents, especially not during the holidays.'

'Go on, you can tell *me* about it.'

'I've been offered a promotion to Head Teacher at Milford-le-Mont Primary.'

'Wow! That's great.'

'No, it's not. I've been in a relationship with the current Head Teacher for eight months, and he doesn't know he's about to lose his job. The school Governors don't know we're a couple; we've managed to keep it quiet. It's such a mess!'

Justin grimaced. 'Nightmare! How have you managed to keep your relationship under wraps? Don't you both drive in together?'

'No. We don't live together. I have my apartment and Desmond house shares. I suggested he move in with me, but he said the people he lives with need his share of the rent, and he doesn't want to let them down.'

Justin was suspicious. 'So, Des is a Head Teacher renting a room in a house?'

'Desmond, not Des. He takes offence when people shorten his name.'

Amy's face dropped, and Justin hit her with a body blow. 'Desmond is married, isn't he?'

The twisted knot in Amy's stomach began to unravel, and her shoulders shook as the sobs came. She stood up and grabbed her bag. 'I need to get out of here.'

*

Back at the lodge, Lottie had taken a shine to Mrs Appleby. Edna didn't move very much. She'd chosen a seat on the end of the sofa nearest the fire and sat there reading a book. She'd been there since breakfast and Lottie could smell the aroma of sherbet lemons whenever Mrs Appleby reached for the bag she had tucked under a cushion. Lottie climbed onto the sofa and sat next to her neighbour as good as gold.

Edna felt a pang of guilt. 'You are a good girl, Lottie. But I can't give you one of my sweets; you might choke on it. What sweets do you like?'

Lottie closed her eyes to think. 'Chocolate

buttons.' Edna reached for her phone and sent a text to Bill:

PLEASE BUY SOME CHOCOLATE
BUTTONS IN THE VILLAGE.

Lottie still had her eyes closed, and Edna had an idea. 'Now, I bet you're wishing for chocolate buttons, aren't you?' Lottie nodded. 'Well, you can open your eyes because now that you've told me, your wish will come true.'

Lottie clapped her hands and looked at Edna expectantly. 'Wishes don't come true as soon as you make them. It can take a little time for the fairies to get your message. Your wish will come true before lunchtime. You won't have very long to wait.'

Lottie grinned. 'Thank you, Mrs Appleby.'

'That's all right, dear. Why don't you go and help your mummy in the kitchen? There's no need to worry about me; I'm happy sitting here reading my book.'

The front door to the lodge flew open and an icy chill encompassed Justin and Amy as they appeared in the lounge laden with bags. It was now Justin who pretended to be happy about anything and everything.

'Hi, Mrs Appleby. Where's everyone?'

There was a shout from the kitchen. 'The men have gone for a walk, and us poor slaves are getting lunch ready.'

Justin laughed. 'You love it in the kitchen, Mum. Amy and I are just going to her room to unpack my shopping. What time's lunch?'

'One o'clock.'

'Great! See you then.'

Amy screwed her eyes up at Justin, and he nudged her along the corridor. When they were inside her room, he shut the door and spoke quietly.

'You've got an hour to pull yourself together. I can't believe you're having an affair with a married man. You should know better, Amy.'

'But I love him, Justin. He'll break up with me if I take his job. If I turn it down, my career will be over before it's even started. I just don't know what to do. I'm a total wreck.'

'It's simple to me. Break it off with him. He'll never leave his wife for you. That way, you'll be free to accept the promotion. He's not worthy of your love. If he's cheating on his wife, he'll cheat on you too.'

Amy collapsed onto her bed and curled up into a ball. Deep down, she knew Justin had a point, but she couldn't help who she fell in love with. She'd never met a man like Desmond before. He'd told her he would leave his wife after the Christmas holidays and Amy trusted him. There wasn't long left to wait until they'd be together. Amy decided love should come before her career. Her mum, Dora, had always told her to follow her heart.

Another icy chill sweeping through the lodge alerted everyone to the return of the men from their walk. Bill found Edna in the lounge and handed her a small bag. 'You got them! Well done. Give them to me and say nothing to no-one. It's our secret.'

Edna jumped up and tip-toed into the dining room. She placed the chocolate buttons on Lottie's plate.

In the kitchen, Carol and Dora were delighted. Justin and Amy were as thick as thieves already. Their teenage friendship had been reignited, and hopes were high for a budding romance.

Lottie dragged Jack down the stairs. 'I'm having chocolate buttons for lunch. I wished for them, and Mrs Appleby promised my wish would come true.'

The children crept into the dining room to the sight of chocolate buttons on Lottie's plate. Jack's eyes were like saucers. 'That's amazing! Mrs Appleby must be a witch.'

Lottie pulled at her brother's jumper. 'Don't tell anyone, Jack, or the magic will go away. Mrs Appleby is our Fairy Godmother.'

Jack nodded and thought of all the things he'd like to wish for. They were so lucky to have a neighbour like Mrs Appleby.

3

SNOWFALL

It was late afternoon when the snow began to fall; it started with the tiniest of flakes that grew within minutes to form huge clusters of drifting prettiness. Edna sat on a window seat with Lottie on her lap. 'When I was a young girl I thought that snowflakes as big as these looked like fairies. Maybe the fairies that brought your chocolate buttons have decided to stay with us for Christmas. They're all flying down from the sky and turning into snow to create a magical winter wonderland.'

Lottie squeezed Edna tightly. 'Yes!! Will the fairies let us turn them into a snowman?'

'Of course, dear. Tomorrow will be the perfect time to make a snowman. There should be enough snow by then. You can dream of that when you go to bed tonight.'

Lottie closed her eyes. 'I wish for a snowman.'

Edna laughed. 'Oh, there's no need to wish for one, dear. You can make one yourself.'

'I want to wish for one.'

*

At four o'clock in the morning, Edna was wide awake. She opened her bedroom curtains, and her heart leapt at the sight of deep snow. She walked around the bed and prodded Bill. 'Wake up, Bill. We need to go outside to make a snowman. Be as quiet as you can. Once we've got it done, we can go back to bed for a couple of hours.

*

It was six-thirty when Lottie let out a scream that ripped through the lodge. 'Mummy! Daddy! There's a snowman outside. He came to visit us in the night. I wished for him.'

The plodding of feet down the stairs woke Justin. The neighbours were soon standing in their dressing gowns looking out of the lounge window. In the centre of the snow-covered lawn stood a six-foot-tall snowman, complete with hat, scarf, coal eyes, carrot nose and twigs for arms. Justin struggled to focus his eyes. Who had gone out to make it in the middle of the night? He was awake until three in the morning. He hadn't seen or heard anyone.

Despite being woken at such an early hour most of the neighbours were in a jubilant mood. Carol and Dora headed for the kitchen to make bacon sandwiches, and Bill and Edna offered to make the teas and coffees. Sharon and Ryan ushered the children upstairs to get dressed in warm clothes ahead of what was going to be a fun-filled morning in the snow.

*

After breakfast, Amy volunteered to load the dishwasher, and Justin stayed behind to help her. Now wide awake, after an unscheduled early start, Amy noticed the dark circles under Justin's eyes. 'Late night?'

'Very late, I'm afraid. It will be an early one tonight.'

'It's your own fault then for looking like a zombie today. You'll get no sympathy from me. You can use our bathroom for a shower instead of going upstairs; Mum and Dad are watching TV in the lounge. Go and tidy yourself up and make sure you put on your new warm clothes. I don't know; I still need to keep an eye on you Justin Lacey after all these years.'

Justin kissed Amy on her cheek, and she squirmed at the touch of his bristly face. 'Thanks for the offer of a bathroom, I'll do as I'm told.'

In the privacy of the steaming shower, Justin had time to think. When he settled down last night at midnight, his hand touched an object down the back of the sofa. He pulled it free. It was a silver bracelet with the name "Millie" carved in an intricate design. A previous guest must have lost it. He'd made a tentative effort to see who Millie was in the Guest Book on the coffee table. On first inspection, he discovered that Millie had stayed in the lodge the previous week. He'd need to let his mum know so that she could contact Guest Services to return the lost property.

In the meantime, Justin put the bracelet on the mantelpiece above the fireplace. Drifting off to sleep was difficult after that. Who was Millie, and why did she stay alone in the lodge for a week? She'd only put *her* name in the "Guests" column, written an excellent review of the lodge and left her email address, which was optional. Justin was intrigued.

'What are you doing in there? I said you could have a shower. You've taken twenty minutes, and that is far longer than any man needs. I want to get dressed. You're on a five-minute warning, or I'm coming in.'

A warm feeling encompassed Justin – it was good having Amy around. 'On my way out! See you outside for a snowball fight in fifteen. That should be enough time for you to make yourself beautiful! Thanks for the use of your bathroom.'

Justin strode into the lounge to see Edna at her usual place on the sofa. Don and Jez had lit a roaring fire and were now standing with Bill looking out of the window. Bill scratched his head. 'I don't know about you two, but I'm getting a bit old for frostbite – my snowball days are over.'

There was a twinkle in Jez's eyes, and he held his shoulders back. Don spoke before one neighbour upset the other. 'You're not much older than us, Bill, the last thing Jez and I would want is to spend a morning trudging around in the cold. How about we all have a game of dominoes?'

Bill rubbed his hands together. 'Now you're talking.'

Carol and Dora clasped their hands around their steaming coffee mugs as they watched the Cassidy family frolicking in the snow. Dora raised an eyebrow. 'I don't know about you, Carol, but now that Amy's grown up I'm done with playing around in the snow. Did you bring any magazines with you? We could join Edna in the lounge.'

A smile swept over Carol's face. 'Good idea. Edna's been doing all right, hasn't she? I never thought she'd eat the Chinese takeaway the other night, but she really tucked in.'

A thud came from the kitchen window, and the women looked up in surprise. More thuds followed – Justin and Amy were outside throwing snowballs at each other. Dora winked at Carol who crossed her fingers and nodded at her best friend. Sometimes actions spoke louder than words.

4

THE BRACELET

That evening, when everyone had retired to bed, Justin sat on the sofa and reached for the Guest Book on the coffee table. Why would Millie leave her email address if she didn't want people to contact her? It had crossed his mind earlier to mention the bracelet to his mother, but he was more than capable of sorting out the return of it on his own, so he emailed Millie:

Hi Millie

My name's Justin, and I'm staying at Seraphina's Lakeside Lodge on the outskirts of Little Marchampton over the Christmas holidays.

I've found a silver bracelet that may belong to you. Please let me know if you've lost a bracelet and, if so, how I can return it to you.

Justin

Within five minutes Justin's iPhone beeped with a "Mail Received" notification:

Hello Justin

I've been looking for my bracelet everywhere! Thank you so much for letting me know it's with you. Please keep hold of it for now. You can return it to me after the holidays.

Have a lovely time at Seraphina's Lakeside Lodge. I would highly recommend it!

Kind regards

Millie

Justin felt at peace. He'd done the right thing. He wondered what Millie looked like. Why had she been staying alone in the lodge? After last night's lack of sleep, Justin drifted off in a sea of dreams.

*

The following afternoon Justin received another email from Millie:

Hello Justin

How are you doing today? I hope you're making the most of the snow. The lodge never looks better than when it's covered in snow. Be careful if you go near the lake, it freezes over quickly, but the ice stays quite thin.

I hope you don't think I'm presumptuous, but are you single?

Kind regards

Millie

A smile lit up Justin's face. So, Millie was young, free, and single after all. This could be fate. Justin wrote back:

Hi Millie

Thanks for the advice about the lake. Do you come here often? Are you local to Little Marchampton?

I hope you have snow where you are too.

Justin

ps I'm very much single.

Millie emailed again:

Hello Justin

I am local to the area. So, yes, we have snow too. Where do you live, and what do you do? Sorry for all the questions. I have an inquisitive nature.

Kind regards

Millie

Justin responded:

Hi Millie

My family's from Milford-le-Mont, which is a five-hour drive south from here. Until recently I was living in Scotland but, following a relationship breakup, I've moved back home until I sort myself out.

Luckily, as a statistician, I am home-based. Lots of video conferences and the odd night away for team meetings, that sort of thing.

What do you do?

Justin

Millie wrote back:

Hello Justin

That's a shame about your relationship breakup. Were you together for long? Why did you break up? Are you heartbroken?

You don't have to answer all of the questions. I just believe it's good to get to know someone right from the start.

I work in the hospitality trade.

Kind regards

Millie

Justin's heart leapt. Millie wanted to get to know him. She was forthright; he'd give that to her. He liked girls with attitude. He'd answer all of Millie's questions – he had nothing to hide. Maybe it was time to be direct with her too:

Hi Millie

We were together for over three years. We broke up because she thought I'd cheated on her. No, I'm not heartbroken, so maybe it was a good thing.

If you're local to here, how about we meet up for a drink? Could you make tomorrow night? I need to return your bracelet, remember.

Justin

There wasn't an immediate response, and Justin felt deflated. He'd pushed it too far. He waited for ten minutes. Nothing. Just over an hour later, his phone beeped:

Hello Justin

Did you cheat on her? Why would she think that?

Millie

Justin sighed; he thought honesty was the best policy. Why were women always so suspicious? What could he say now?

Hi Millie

I'm a decent guy. I would never cheat on a woman. A drunken friend of mine started a rumour that was all. I was hurt and annoyed that the girl I had been going out with for over three years believed it. So, when she ended things, I didn't put up a fight to get her back. It's as simple as that.

Justin

It was ten minutes before Millie responded.

Hello Justin

Sorry for sounding harsh. A drink would be lovely. I'll see you in the pub on the High Street at seven-thirty tomorrow night if that is acceptable to you?

Kind regards

Millie

Justin let out a sigh of relief before writing back:

Hi Millie

See you then!

Justin

*ps I'll be holding your bracelet so that you know who
I am.*

5

SURPRISES IN STORE

Justin arrived at the pub at seven-fifteen. He'd told all the neighbours the story of Millie's bracelet and that he was popping out to return it to her, everyone seemed pleased that he was doing a good deed. Justin didn't mention the grilling she'd given him or the excitement he felt at the chance of a potential new relationship. He'd be asking Millie questions tonight. All he knew about her was that she lived locally and was in the hospitality trade. She must be single, though, or she wouldn't have asked so many questions.

Justin bought a pint and sat down at a table next to the window. He'd be able to see Millie arrive from there. He didn't account for the tall blonde girl who was standing at the bar to walk over to join him. 'Mind if I join you?' Tall blond girl sat down and placed her wine glass on a beer mat.

'Are you Millie?'

'No.'

Justin was speechless. He was excited about meeting Millie, but now this girl that looked like an angel had appeared from nowhere. Her sparkling blue eyes made his stomach lurch. What should he do? He doubted very much that Millie would be as stunning as the girl now sitting opposite him sipping her glass of wine. It wouldn't hurt to have a chat before Millie turned up.

'Do you come here often?'

'Bad chat up line.'

Justin squirmed. 'I presume you live locally?'

'Yes, I'm very local.'

Justin felt extremely uncomfortable. Tall blonde girl's eyes danced with merriment and Millie was due to arrive any second. He had a sinking feeling that he could end up with neither woman by the end of the evening. He had to make a choice. Justin picked up his pint and stood up.

'I'm sorry, but I'm meeting someone at seven-thirty. She should be here any minute. It won't look good if I'm seen chatting to you. Please excuse me; I'll wait up at the bar.'

Tall blonde girl caught hold of Justin's hand, and her bracelet shone under the artificial light. It was silver and the same design as Millie's. Justin's heart pounded as he reached for the bracelet in his pocket.

'Ah, you remembered to bring it. Millie will be pleased.'

Justin sat down again. 'You know Millie?'

'Yes, I do, and she won't be meeting you tonight.'

'Why not?'

'Because fifty-five-year-old women don't take kindly to getting chatted up via email by losers such as you. Please give me the bracelet.'

Justin handed the bracelet over, and the angel that had turned into a wild woman downed her drink and left the pub.

*

Back at the lodge, the children were in bed, Sharon was in the bath and Ryan was keen to have a quiet word with Amy. He'd been bottling it up for weeks, but after two glasses of Merlot with dinner and now a pint of beer, he couldn't resist ruffling a few feathers.

'Have you heard the news about old Dessie? You teachers must enjoy a bit of gossip in the staff room. It was Sharon that told me. The right and proper married Head Teacher is having an affair.'

Amy wanted the floor to open up and swallow her right there and then. She felt nauseous, her face had drained of colour, and her legs felt like jelly. She couldn't speak or even move. Ryan didn't notice as he flicked through the channels on the TV and continued to pummel Amy to the ground with his revelations.

'Mind you, Lizzie Do-Do Whatsit – I can never remember her posh name – is a yummy mummy in any man's eyes. Sharon says the parents have a petition going to get him removed from post. He's got a couple more weeks of illicit fun; then he'll be hit by a ton of bricks. Cheaters always get their comeuppance in the end.'

Sharon called down from the landing. 'Ryan! Can you come upstairs and read these two another story? They just won't settle tonight. I need to dry my hair.'

Ryan jumped up. 'Coming, my dearest.' He winked at Amy. 'If the teachers don't know what's going on yet then best not mention it. Just wait for the fireworks in January.'

When Justin entered the lounge, he was shocked to see Amy sitting on the sofa looking crestfallen. 'What's happened?'

Amy blew her nose. 'I need to get to my bedroom; I can hardly breathe. My legs feel weak, and I don't want to cause a fuss. Can you help me?'

Justin could hear his mother and Dora in the kitchen. Don, Jez, and Bill were in the dining room playing cards, and the other neighbours were upstairs. The coast was clear. 'Stand up and put your arm around me, I'll help you to your room. Are you sure you don't need a doctor?'

'What day is it?'

'Wednesday.'

'No. The date.'

'The twenty-third of December.'

'Good. We've just got time.'

'Time for what?'

'For me to dump Dessie boy and to accept his job. Everywhere will shut from tomorrow lunchtime until the New Year.'

Justin kissed Amy on the cheek. 'That's the best news I've had all year!'

Don saw the couple embrace in the hallway and nudged Jez who gave a thumbs-up sign. Things could be on for a summer wedding. The Lacey's and Pritchard's were soon to be united.

6

CHRISTMAS EVE

Millie was less than impressed with her daughter. 'I can't believe you did that last night. You can be so hard at times. I'd done all the research and Justin is the perfect match for you.'

'Oh, Mother! You are a nightmare. Why don't you just leave me to sort out my own love life.'

'If I leave it to you, Seraphina, you'll end up with a loser like your father. No way will I let that happen. I've had to bring up two children on my own for twenty-two years. You were just three when he ran off. At least marrying a rich cheater meant we weren't left penniless when he sailed off into the sunset with that actress. Do you know he left her after two years; he's on his fourth wife now?'

'Yes, Mother. I read the newspaper gossip columns too – you haven't spoken about him for years. This Justin guy has opened up old wounds for you. If you hadn't stayed in the lodge last week and lost your bracelet, you wouldn't be in such a state now.'

'Well, I needed a change of scenery and a bit of space. It's rare that one of the lodges is available so close to Christmas, I enjoyed a week of solitude.'

Seraphina looked out of the window. The lake was freezing over. She was pleased to see the enormous snowman that had appeared on the other side of the lake a few days ago was still standing tall and proud. She couldn't remember the last time she had made a snowman. Her brother was too old now to help her. He was busy with his job, leaving Seraphina and Millie to manage the lodges.

'Put your coat and hat on, Mum. You'll need a scarf and gloves too. We're going outside to make a snowman. It needs to be at least as big as the one on the other side of the lake.'

*

After lunch, Amy and Justin offered to take the children out for some fresh air. Amy was feeling revitalised. She'd accepted the job! Amy had also well and truly floored old Dessie, and no doubt spoiled his Christmas. Just wait until he heard that she'd be replacing him. That would be the icing on the cake!

Justin was thrilled for Amy, but tall blonde girl was stuck in his mind. She was rude, she was arrogant, but more than anything, she was beautiful. He shook his head to try to clear all thoughts of her. The likelihood of meeting her again was next to zero.

Lottie jumped up and down. 'The snowman's got a girlfriend!'

Jack's eyes lit up, and Justin came out of his trance to see a snowman standing tall the other side of the lake wearing a pink hat and scarf.

Amy clapped her hands in delight. 'Come along, children. We need to walk a whole lap of the lake so that we can get a better view of Mrs Snowman. How exciting is that?'

Seraphina heard the squeals outside and peered out of the lounge window. She darted behind a curtain at the sight of Justin with a young woman and two children outside. Millie was in the study and witnessed the same scene. She couldn't help but send an email:

Hello Justin

Thank you for returning my bracelet. You've heard by now that I'm much too old for you. I was just wondering who the girl with brown hair is and the two young children? It's a lovely afternoon for a walk.

Kind regards

Millie

Justin's head spun round. Millie could see him! There were several lodges around the lake. Was she inside a lodge? Justin responded:

Hi Millie

Sorry for trying to chat you up. I'm on holiday with my parents and our neighbours. Girl with brown hair's family live next door to my family, and the children belong to our neighbours. Before you ask, girl with brown hair is not a love interest.

I think it's about time I asked you a question. Who was the girl that met me in the pub last night? Is she single?

Justin

Millie's heart skipped a beat. Justin was interested in Seraphina. She wrote back:

Hello Justin

She's my daughter. She's hot-headed and stubborn but has the kindest of hearts, and she's very much single.

Love Millie x

Justin couldn't contain a broad smile. Seraphina

wondered who he was messaging on his phone. Millie saw Justin's delight too and read his next message:

Hi Millie

Do I have your approval to take your daughter on a date? If so, you will need to help me arrange it as I think she'll turn me down flat.

Regards, Justin

Millie started to write back:

Hello Justin

You do have my approval, and I'll arrange the date. Are you available at four o'clock . . .

The door to the lodge slammed, and Seraphina strode outside to talk to Justin, who was standing alone playing with his phone; Amy had headed back with the children before they got too cold. She stood with hands on hips. 'Not only did you try to chat up my mother, but you are also here on holiday in one of our lodges with your wife and children!'

The silver bracelet caught Justin's eye again, and he reached out to hold tall blonde girl's hand, he read her name out loud: 'Seraphina.'

Seraphina pulled her hand away. 'Yes, I'm Seraphina and my mother, Millie, owns the lodges. She is divorced, I am single, and you are married!'

Millie watched the kerfuffle going on outside; Seraphina was her own worst enemy at times. Justin kept his calm. 'Your mother has already established my credentials, and she is well aware that I am single too. You need to apologise to me now for jumping to the wrong conclusion.'

Seraphina shook her head as a redness crept up her neck and exploded over her pretty face. 'I never apologise. There's something about you being here that disturbs me. I can't work out what it is.'

'So, you have feelings for me?'

'Not like that!'

Seraphina turned around and stormed back inside the lodge. Millie deleted her current email and wrote another one:

Hello Justin

I'll apologise on Seraphina's behalf. My daughter is her own worst enemy. You have my approval; I'll do my best to get you hers. It could take a while, though. Enjoy Christmas!

Love Millie x

Seraphina bounded into the study. 'Did you see that? He's got a wife and children! I saw it with my own eyes, and he still tried to deny it. I'll never trust a man, not after what my father did to you.'

'Oh, darling. There are lots of men out there who are not like your father. Justin's on holiday with his neighbours. He was childminding, and he's got no interest in that girl with brown hair. You make things difficult for yourself, you really do. Justin won't put up with your behaviour forever. Stop being so rude to him and try to be nice.'

7

CHRISTMAS MORNING

Lottie and Jack were awake by five o'clock. They unwrapped the presents in the stockings hanging from the bunk beds.

Jack held up a little wooden boat. 'Wow! Mr Lacey makes these. I've seen him painting them in his shed.'

Lottie had a boat in her stocking too. 'Mr Lacey must be one of Santa's little helpers.'

'I'm going to see if my boat floats in the bath.'

'Wait for me! I'll bring my boat too.'

Jack pushed the plug into the hole and turned on the tap. Cold water began to fill the bath. By the time the water level was at six inches, the boats started to float. The water kept rising, and the children were delighted to watch their boats bobbing around.

Edna awoke with a start. She had a feeling that all was not right in the lodge. She had to check on Lottie and Jack. By the time Edna reached the bathroom, the water was dripping over the side of the bath, and Jack was struggling to turn the tap off. She quickly turned the tap off, pulled the plug out and mopped up the first signs of a flood with a towel.

Lottie and Jack stood in silence. They clung onto their boats waiting to be punished. 'I take it you both know how naughty that was?'

The children nodded. 'You must never do that again, and never turn on the hot taps without the help of an adult. You could have been scolded. Hot water is dangerous. Do you understand?'

The children nodded again. 'As it's Christmas Day, I won't tell anyone about this mishap. Just promise me you'll go back to bed and not get up until eight o'clock.'

Lottie's eyes filled with tears. 'I don't know when it's eight o'clock.'

Jack grabbed his sister's hand. 'I do. Thank you, Mrs Appleby.'

Jack shut their bedroom door before whispering. 'We'll stay in bed until Mummy and Daddy come to get us. Mrs Appleby really is our Fairy Godmother, isn't she? The bathroom floor nearly got wet. She saved us just in time.'

Edna tidied the bathroom and went back to bed.

Ryan turned over and looked at the alarm clock; it was eight-forty-five. Where were the children? They never had a lie-in on Christmas Day. He woke Sharon up, and they headed down the landing in trepidation. They needn't have worried; Jack and Lottie were sitting up in their beds with wrapping paper strewn across the floor.

Ryan held the ladder for Jack to climb down. 'I can't believe how good you two are. You didn't want to wake the neighbours, did you?'

Jack looked at the floor. 'No, we didn't.'

Lottie clung onto her boat. 'We've worked out that Mr Lacey is one of Santa's little helpers.'

Sharon and Ryan burst out laughing. Sharon drew back the curtains. 'Come along, you two; you need to come downstairs. Santa came down the chimney last night, and he may have left some more presents in the lounge.'

Bill left Edna in bed. She said she was feeling a bit off colour. Edna wasn't sure if it was the early morning incident that had unsettled her, or if it was something else. She just couldn't shake off an overwhelming feeling of doom and gloom.

Downstairs the turkey was in the oven, the lodge was filled with Christmas music, and the view from the windows of a thick covering of fresh snow brought smiles to everyone's faces. Edna's presents were placed in a pile for her to unwrap later while the neighbours let the holiday mood take over. Don kissed Carol under a sprig of mistletoe; Jez and Dora danced around like a couple of teenagers – much to Amy's embarrassment – and Justin challenged Bill to a game of pool in the games room.

Sharon and Ryan were sat on the floor with their children playing with a racing car set when Carol called for help in the kitchen. Sharon got up, and Dora stopped dancing, giving Jez the chance to play with Ryan. Jack wandered into the games room, and Bill moved a chair next to the pool table so that Jack could stand on it and have a go at potting a few balls.

Edna was restless; she couldn't stop thinking about her mother. It had been a worry throughout her childhood that her mother would die young. So, it was no surprise to ten-year-old Edna when Mystic Marigold Mayweather collapsed in a heap over her crystal ball at the age of thirty-two. Edna decided there and then to suppress her psychic ability. As far as she was concerned, it wasn't a gift – it was a burden. Edna had even predicted the date and time of her mother's sad demise – she never told her, there was no point. Marigold's destiny had been written in the stars.

From that day forward, Edna managed to control her thoughts and feelings and hide them away at the back of her mind. She didn't get involved in other people's business. She kept herself to herself as much as possible. But, today, however hard she tried to ignore her instinct she couldn't – Lottie was in danger.

Edna jumped out of bed and threw open the doors to her balcony. Lottie was carrying her boat and heading across the snow towards the lake. Edna flew out of her bedroom onto the landing before screaming: 'Lottie's by the lake, she's going to drown!'

Justin was nearest the front door, he ran across the snow, followed by Ryan. Edna rushed down the stairs and tripped half-way. Don and Jez ran to her aid.

Lottie was quick. She was determined to see if her boat would float on the lake, but when she reached the edge, it had frozen over. Lottie bent down and touched the ice – it was hard. She'd been to an ice rink with her parents and Jack; they'd had great fun. Mummy had pushed her around on a penguin and Jack had skated on the ice himself with the help of a polar bear. Lottie couldn't see any plastic animals on the lake. There was a fir tree that was blocking her view, so she stepped onto the ice to see around the corner.

Ryan ran down the snow-covered lawn screaming Lottie's name, and Justin lurched forward to grab the small child. He slipped and couldn't reach Lottie before the ice cracked and she slid through.

Ryan caught up with Justin to witness Lottie being lifted to safety. A sobbing Ryan cradled his daughter as Justin pulled Seraphina out of the lake. She'd appeared from behind the trees and was now soaking wet and trembling. He lifted the annoying woman into his arms before calling over to Ryan: 'We need to get these two into the lodge as soon as possible.'

Seraphina thumped Justin as her teeth chattered. 'I don't need any help.'

Justin ignored her. He couldn't believe how heavy she was. He guessed that was due to her sodden clothes. As far as he was concerned, he would have carried her whatever weight she was to wherever she needed to go. Right now, she needed to get into the warm, and so did he. There hadn't been time to grab a jacket.

Dora rushed into the downstairs bathroom to get towels for everyone, and Carol tried to persuade Edna that they should phone for an ambulance. 'I've only bruised my arm, Carol. Jez managed to catch me. It was Don who grabbed my wrist.'

Don handed Seraphina a mug of hot chocolate and raised an eyebrow at Justin. He wondered who the girl was. She had just turned up from nowhere.

Justin reached for his phone to email Millie. He turned to the drenched heroine and said: 'I'll let your mother know where you are.'

Carol shot a glance at Don, and Seraphina held her hand out to Justin. 'If you lend me your phone, I'll call her.'

Seraphina dialled Millie's number. 'Hi, Mother. I'm in a bit of a predicament. I sort of fell into the lake, and I'm at the lodge opposite. Can you pick me up please and bring Danny with you so he can check out a couple of casualties? Great. See you in ten.'

8

CHRISTMAS LUNCH

Edna ate her Christmas lunch with a fork. Her left wrist was severely sprained and had been bandaged up by Doctor Danny – Seraphina's brother. She had bruised her hip too. The neighbours were more than happy for Edna and Bill to eat their meal in the comfort of the lounge.

Bill glanced sideways at Edna. 'Is there something you want to tell me, dear?'

Edna shook her head.

'I've always thought there was something a bit magical about you. You can predict things, can't you?'

'No, I can't.'

'Yes, you can. I've noticed it over the years, and just today you predicted the bathroom was about to be flooded and that little Lottie was in danger.'

'How did you know about the bathroom?'

'I crept out of bed to see where you had gone.'

'Oh!'

'You never mention your mother. Could she predict things too?'

'I'm not a witch!'

Jack and Lottie appeared in the doorway of the lounge with a plate of mince pies. Jack spoke first. 'I said you were a witch, but you're not really one.'

Lottie climbed onto the sofa next to Edna. 'We know who you are.'

Edna swallowed hard. 'Who am I?'

'You're our Fairy Godmother.'

Jack sat on the floor at Edna's feet. 'Everyone knows you're special. You knew Lottie was in trouble and you knew I couldn't turn the bath tap off. We owned up to that just now. Mummy and Daddy sent us in here to thank you and to bring you these.' Jack held the plate aloft, and Bill took hold of it.

Edna smiled. 'Now run along you two, get back to all the fun in the other room, and try to stay out of trouble.'

Edna turned to face Bill and chose her words carefully. 'My mother was a clairvoyant who collapsed over her crystal ball and died when she was thirty-two. I predicted it, but I didn't stop it.'

Bill patted his wife's knee. 'It sounds to me that you couldn't have stopped that. You prevented two disasters today, though. You should view your powers as a gift, not a burden. Why don't I buy you a crystal ball?'

Edna chuckled. 'I don't want a crystal ball, Bill. I don't need one. You've just made me feel so much better. I should have told you years ago.'

Jack and Lottie ran back into the dining room, and Don turned to Jez. 'I've always had a question mark over Edna. There's something mysterious about her. After what happened today, I think she may be able to see into the future. I'd be keen to know if that's the case. I wonder if she predicts the Grand National winner each year?'

Jez rubbed his hands together. 'Mystic Edna would do well at Milford-le-Mont Summer Fair.'

Dora interrupted the conversation. 'Stop gossiping you two. You sound like a couple of old women.'

Justin helped Carol clear the plates from the table. When they were alone in the kitchen, she cornered him. 'You've refused to talk about it yet, and I know that this morning's events were quite frightening, but you need to tell me how you know that girl and her mother.'

Justin sighed; the truth would come out sometime. 'The girl is called Seraphina.'

Carol's eyes widened. 'That's the name of the lodge.'

Justin nodded. 'Correct. Her mother owns the lodges, and she stayed in this one last week. She lost her bracelet down the back of the sofa. I found it and returned it to her via her daughter. They live in the lodge opposite and before you ask, I've tried to get Seraphina to go on a date, but she's as obnoxious as they come. There's no chance she will go out with me.'

'But what about Amy? Dora and I had always hoped our two families would be united.'

An idea hit Justin from out of the blue. It was perfect, just perfect! 'I tell you what, Mum. I'll take Amy into town tomorrow lunchtime. We can have a drink in the pub.'

'Ah, that's lovely, Justin. Dora will be pleased.'

'That's good then. It's important to keep the neighbours happy.'

Carol hugged her son and cut him an extra-large slice of Christmas cake.

*

It was nearly five o'clock before Millie read Justin's latest message:

Hi Millie

I hope you're having a good Christmas Day, after this morning's unfortunate start. Your daughter was quite the heroine.

As it's very unlikely that Seraphina will accept an offer to meet me at the pub, could you please arrange for Danny to take her there for a drink at noon tomorrow? I'll bring my neighbour, Amy, along and, hopefully, we can all bump into one another. It's worth a try.

Regards, Justin

Millie replied:

Hello Justin

That's a great idea. I'll sort it out. Amy seems like a very nice young lady. I managed to get a quick chat with her earlier. She advised me that she's a school teacher and she's single.

FYI Danny's single too.

Good luck tomorrow.

Love Millie x

9

BOXING DAY

Considering her sprained wrist and bruised hip, Edna was up bright and early and trying to make pancakes with one hand. Bill was rushing around helping his wife when Don popped his head into the kitchen. 'Need any help, you two? I haven't pulled my weight in the kitchen yet. It won't be long before Carol starts nagging me.'

Edna laughed. 'Carol never nags you. You've got a good wife there, Don.'

Don took a step backwards. Was that Edna in the kitchen? She'd never spoken so many words to him in one go. She also didn't have that haunted look about her that made him try to avoid her at all costs.

Edna whisked the pancake mixture while Bill held onto the bowl. 'I have an excellent feeling about today.

Things are taking a turn for the better.'

Don scratched his chin. 'So, you're not predicting any disasters today then?'

'No. No disasters today.'

Justin was showering in Edna and Bill's en-suite. Edna had suggested he use it as they were both up and ready early. Without a bedroom of his own, Justin was always on the lookout for somewhere to wash and change. Justin couldn't stop thinking about Seraphina. He hoped she'd be nicer to him today. He was also intrigued as to why she was on the wrong side of the lake yesterday morning. As it turned out, it was the right side to save Lottie, but why was Seraphina there? Had she gone for a morning stroll trying to catch a glimpse of him? Justin smiled at that thought. Lunchtime couldn't come quick enough.

*

Amy turned up the collar of her jacket against the strong wind. She could see her parents waving out of the lodge window. 'You are going to be in so much trouble, Justin Lacey. You're making our parents believe something is going on between us by using me so that you can meet up with Seraphina.'

'I need all the help I can get. It's the first time that I have a girl's mother on board before the girl will even look me in the eye. I don't know what I've done, but

Seraphina's taken offence to me from the start.'

'Sounds like she's a wise woman. I'm beginning to like her. Having a dishy brother also works in her favour.'

'That's more like it, Amy. The four of us could have some fun. I saw Doctor Danny take a backwards glance at you when he left the lodge yesterday.'

'Is that all I got? A backwards glance!'

'Well, it's a start. Millie says he's single and you've got her approval.'

Amy tutted. 'Talk about "meddling mothers", where would we be without them?'

Justin slowed his walking pace. 'Keep your head down. They're in front of us. Let's hope they don't see us before they go in.'

Amy wrapped her scarf around her mouth before giggling. Christmas with the neighbours wasn't turning out too bad after all.

Justin pulled the pub door open and let Amy walk through first. His eyes darted around the room before he felt a light hand on his shoulder. 'Hello Justin, fancy seeing you here.' He remained rooted to the spot at the sight of an amiable Seraphina.

'Oh, hi, Seraphina. I've just popped out for a quick

one with Amy. You've met Amy, haven't you?'

Amy and Seraphina smiled at each other, and Danny held out his hand to Justin. 'Sorry I didn't introduce myself yesterday. It was all a bit of a rush. I'm Danny, Seraphina's brother.'

Justin shook Danny's hand. 'Hi Danny, I'm Justin, and this is Amy. She used to be the girl next door, but we both live away from our parents now.' Justin lowered his eyes. 'Well, that's not entirely true, I'm back home again for the moment until I find a new place.'

Seraphina couldn't help but sense Justin's awkwardness. Had *she* done that to him? He was much more confident and charming when she saw him in the pub last week. Her mother's words disturbed her: *Justin won't put up with your behaviour forever. Stop being so rude to him and try to be nice.*

Compared to last week, Seraphina felt surprisingly calm. She'd had a sinking feeling when the neighbours from Milford-le-Mont had moved into the opposite lodge, and she couldn't explain why. The pressure had lifted now, though, and she was keen to get to know them better. She turned to Amy. 'Are you enjoying your holiday in Little Marchampton?'

Amy unravelled her scarf and shoved her gloves into her jacket pocket. 'Very much so. The lodge is lovely. I'm in one of the downstairs bedrooms; poor Justin is on the sofa. Aren't you, Justin?'

Justin coughed. 'I came along at the last minute. There was a change of plan.'

Seraphina smiled. 'Well, it's a good job you've been sleeping on the sofa, otherwise you may never have found our mother's bracelet.'

Amy held out her hand to admire Seraphina's bracelet. 'May I? Justin tells me it's the same design as your mother's. It's so unusual. It really catches the light.'

Justin stood at the bar with Danny. 'How long has your mother owned the lodges?'

'It must be over twenty years now. She had them built one at a time; the one we live in is the oldest. I have to admire her for having the vision to grow the business when she was left stranded with two young children. Our father was a loser – Seraphina would tell you the same. We've disowned him.'

Justin was surprised by Danny's candidness.

The girls found a table and sat down. Amy hung her jacket on the back of her chair, she turned around before speaking, 'Justin's really rather nice, you know. He's always been a good friend to me.'

'Have you ever dated him?'

'No. I tend to go for bad guys.'

Seraphina raised her eyebrows. Amy didn't look the type to go for bad guys.

The men placed the drinks on the table, and Amy chattered away. 'Something weird has been going on in our lodge. I didn't think everyone would get along for a whole two weeks but, so far, so good. You agree with me, Justin, don't you?'

'I never thought about it. I just turned up.'

Amy leant forward, clasping her glass. 'Well, everyone thought that Edna Appleby would be a nightmare to live with, but she's really come into her own. The children love her and, apart from spending most of yesterday morning in bed, she's made a big effort to join in.'

Danny glanced at Seraphina, then looked at Amy. 'Does Mrs Appleby spend time in bed during the day very often?'

Amy closed her eyes to think. 'Well, when I used to live at home, her bedroom curtains would be drawn on the odd occasions. Mum always used to say: "Edna's having one of her bad days". It was extraordinary yesterday though. She jumped out of bed when she thought Lottie was in danger. It was a good thing Seraphina was nearby to save her from drowning.'

Seraphina kicked Danny under the table, and he chose not to ask any more questions on that subject. 'Well, my sister always turns up in the right place at the right time. We can rely on her to do that. What do you both have planned for the next few days?'

Amy looked at Justin who shrugged his shoulders, so Danny continued, 'Our Mother is going away for New Year so Seraphina and I thought we should throw a party.' Seraphina kicked Danny again; that was the first she had heard of it. Danny checked his watch. 'She'll be in the air right now; her flight took off ten minutes ago. Why don't we aim for a party tomorrow night?'

A smiling Justin nudged Amy. 'I'm up for that, are you?'

Amy grinned. 'Most definitely!'

'Great! Let's aim for eight o'clock. Make sure you bring torches with you. It's floodlit around the lake, but there are still some dark spots on the walk from your lodge to ours.'

The sun in the sky soon made way for dark clouds. Seraphina finished her drink. 'There's more snow on the way. We should start to head back.'

Danny jumped up. 'It's been great meeting you both. See you tomorrow night at ours.'

As soon as the pub door closed, Justin punched the air. 'She was nice to me – and we have a date!'

Amy pulled on her jacket. 'I must admit I quite like Seraphina. Danny's not too bad either.'

When they reached the lodge, Carol shivered at the sight of them. 'It's snowing again!'

Justin shook his jacket outside. 'Yes, Mum. Oh and, before we forget, we won't need dinner tomorrow night, we're going out.'

10

A BIG WISH

After breakfast the following morning, Jack wandered into the lounge to find Mrs Appleby. 'I want to make a wish.'

Edna put her book down. 'What do you want to wish for, Jack?'

'A dinosaur.'

Edna took in a sharp intake of breath. That wish was outside of her remit. She'd hoped the boy would wish for a balloon or some sweets; she could just about run to that.

'Dinosaurs are extinct.'

'But you're our Fairy Godmother. You make our

wishes come true.'

Jack's eyes filled with tears, and Edna knew she had to be creative. 'Well, I'll see what I can do.'

Jack ran off up the stairs to tell Lottie, and Edna knocked on Amy's room. 'I need a bit of help. Jack has wished for a dinosaur. Do you know how to make one?'

Amy laughed. 'We make everything at school; I'm sure I could give it a try.'

Edna rubbed her wrist. It was much better than a couple of days ago and her hip, although shocking in colour, had improved too. 'Well, I'd best take a trip into the village to get supplies.'

Amy looked up from painting her toenails. 'If you give me half an hour I'll come with you.'

'No need. I'm quite capable of buying a few sheets of cardboard and some glue. I'll be back for lunch.'

Edna wrapped up warm and pulled on her fur-lined boots before venturing out into the cold. She headed down the track to the village to find Seraphina walking towards her.

'It's Seraphina, isn't it? I'm Edna Appleby – the one who fell down the stairs.'

'Oh, hello, Mrs Appleby. What a strange start to

Christmas Day that was. I had a bad feeling leading up to that for weeks.'

'Me too, dear. It was so bad that I did a silly thing and went to bed, hoping it would go away.'

'I do that sometimes. It's like having a premonition, isn't it? Knowing something bad is going to happen but not being able to do anything about it.'

'But you did do something about it, Seraphina. You were in the right place at the right time. I was a coward and hid under my duvet until the very last minute when I panicked and fell down the stairs.'

Edna smiled, and Seraphina laughed. 'What a pair we are? Why are you heading into the village on a Sunday? There's nothing open. If you need some bread or milk, I can drop some round.'

Edna's shoulders drooped. 'That's the most terrible news. I need to make a dinosaur. Little Jack has wished for one; he thinks I'm his Fairy Godmother. This will blow my cover!'

Seraphina linked arms with Edna. 'Come with me. I've got an idea that should turn you into the best Fairy Godmother ever.'

Edna sat by the fire in Seraphina's lounge, sipping a cup of tea. 'Your home is lovely, dear. Is your mother around?'

Seraphina raised her eyes to the ceiling. 'For some reason, my mother and brother are colluding to fix me up with Justin. My mother has suddenly gone away until after the New Year, and my brother's delighted about it. That leaves me home alone with Danny, who has invited Justin and Amy here tonight for a party. They are going to be so disappointed when they turn up.'

'Doctor Danny?'

'Yes, Doctor Danny.'

'Oh, I can see where your mother's coming from there then. Justin is soft on you, and Danny has eyes for Amy. She's very clever, your mother.'

Seraphina blushed. 'I can't let my guard down around men. My father treated my mother so badly that we disowned him. I've not met a good man yet.'

'Oh, yes, you have. Justin is perfect for you. I've got a premonition – a good one – about you two.'

'Really? I've sort of got a good feeling too.'

'Well, let that feeling flourish, my dear. You can't spend your whole life waiting for the worst to happen. Trust me; I've done that. Now that I've stopped, I feel so much better.'

Seraphina gazed into the fire. I feel we're on the same wavelength, Mrs Appleby.'

'Oh, please call me Edna. Now, you must let me know your idea that will turn me into the best Fairy Godmother ever.'

Seraphina ran upstairs – she returned with a dinosaur costume. Edna clapped her hands, then held onto her throbbing wrist. 'Oh, my goodness! That will be perfect.'

'Danny bought this for Halloween a few years back. I'm sure I'll fit into it.'

Edna shrieked with delight. 'You're going to be the dinosaur?'

'Why not? If it makes Jack's wish come true, it will be very worthwhile.'

'When shall we do it?'

Seraphina looked at the clock on the wall. 'Well, it's twelve-thirty now. What time do you all have lunch?'

'One o'clock. I should start heading back before I'm late.'

'Shall we aim for two o'clock so that everyone's still around? The children won't go out before that will they?'

Edna stood up and hugged her new friend. 'You're a good girl, Seraphina. Two o'clock it is!'

Bill opened the door for Edna to enter. 'Where have you been? Amy said you'd gone shopping, but the shops are shut.'

Edna put a finger to her lips. 'I'm on Fairy Godmother duties.'

Amy walked into the hall. 'I completely forgot that it's Sunday. I'm sorry you had a wasted journey,' Amy lowered her voice, 'we'll have to make a dinosaur later in the week.'

*

Edna kept an eye on the clock in the dining room; it was approaching two o'clock. All of a sudden Lottie let out a scream and pointed to the window. Everyone turned around to see a dinosaur plodding along through the snow. Jack clung to his father and buried his face in his chest. Bill glanced at Edna, who looked worried by the children's reaction.

The dinosaur turned around and headed towards the window. Jack and Lottie watched through their fingers. The dinosaur waved and danced around. Lottie jumped up. 'I want to go outside!'

Jack stood in front of Edna, who held her good hand up for a high-five. 'You're the best Fairy Godmother ever. Wait until they hear about this at school!' He looked over at Amy. 'You'll tell everyone too, won't you, Miss Pritchard? A dinosaur came to see us because I wished for it!'

There were smiles all around the dining table, and the adults discretely winked or gave Edna a "thumbs up" sign.

The neighbours headed to the lounge window where they saw the dinosaur waving as it walked around the lake. It was some way into the distance when it slipped and landed head-first into the snow. It didn't get up. Everyone gasped and looked at one another. Edna swallowed hard. 'I think the dinosaur needs a bit of help. Justin's the best person to help a dinosaur with a sore head. Off you go, Justin. Quick! Make sure it's nothing serious.'

Justin felt Edna's angst and strode around the lake as fast as he could. When he reached the dinosaur, he saw Seraphina's eyes inside the head. He burst out laughing.

'Don't worry. I'm not injured. My pride's a bit dented, but that's about it. I can't get up, though, without a bit of help. Just make sure my head doesn't fall off in the process.'

Justin helped the dinosaur up. It turned around and waved to the neighbours before hiding behind a fir tree until the onlookers dispersed.

'Have they stopped watching now?'

'Yes.'

'OK. I'll head off home. See you at eight.'

11

THE PRIVATE PARTY

Danny saw Amy and Justin approaching from a distance. It was a good idea to advise them to bring torches, apart from the safety aspect, it gave him the opportunity to spot Amy and intercept her before she got to the lodge. The couple were just a few feet away now, and Danny jumped out of the shadows. Amy shrieked. 'What on earth are you doing? You gave me the fright of my life. Why aren't you inside hosting the party?'

Danny shrugged his shoulders. 'There's no party to host. It was just a plan of mine to get Justin and Seraphina together. The only problem is, you and I are now spare parts. We can't go in the lodge, or we'll be a couple of wallflowers intruding on a nice romantic evening for two.'

Amy stamped her foot – her very cold foot – and folded her arms. Danny smiled at Justin. 'You should head over to the lodge, Seraphina's inside. I'll take care of Amy.' Justin's heart pounded, and he did as he was told.

Danny took hold of Amy's torch. 'Thanks for bringing this, we'll need it where we're going.' Danny headed down a narrow track away from the lake with Amy in hot pursuit.

'Where *are* we going?'

'Where would a bad guy take you?'

Amy frowned. 'Seraphina told you I go for bad guys, didn't she?'

'I might have heard a rumour.'

'Well, a bad guy would try to keep me hidden and all to himself. So, you're showing signs of being a bad guy already.'

'Have you had much success with bad guys?'

'No.'

Danny glanced over his shoulder. 'Maybe you should try good guys then.'

*

Justin read the sign on the wall of the lodge: "Millie's

Lakeside Lodge". He smiled; he could have guessed the name. Seraphina opened the door. 'I have to apologise for my brother. There is no party. On top of that, he's been missing for half an hour. Where's Amy?'

Justin smiled. 'We've been set up. Danny and Amy have gone off together so that we can be alone.'

Despite the flickering candlelight, Justin noticed Seraphina's cheeks turn pink. 'Well, what are we going to do?'

'I don't know about you, but I'm hungry.'

Seraphina headed for the kitchen. 'Will spaghetti carbonara do?'

'Perfect.'

*

The narrow track opened up, and Amy found herself standing before an open carriage, with driver and two white horses wearing sleigh bells. She threw a hand to her mouth.

'Don't tell me you're scared of horses.'

Amy shook her head. 'I'm scared of nice guys.'

Danny helped Amy into the carriage and shut the door. He reached for a fleece blanket and tucked it around their legs. With the passengers safely seated, the horses set off at a trot, and a tour of the village commenced. Danny put an arm around Amy to shield her from the cold, and she clasped his free gloved hand with her own.

After circling the village green three times, the carriage stopped outside the village hall. Danny opened the door and helped Amy down the folding steps. He spoke to the driver, and the carriage pulled away. Danny took a key out of his pocket. 'My grandparents owed me a favour, so I called it in.'

Amy laughed. 'Why did your grandparents owe you a favour?'

'I'm on the Board of the Village Hall Committee. My grandparents asked me to vote for their idea of Tea Dances. Anyway, they've been a great success. I thought we could try out a bit of dancing in private as the room will be set up ready for tomorrow.'

Not only was the room set up, but Danny's grandmother had also left a feast of sandwiches and savouries in the kitchen. A plateful of pasties caught Amy's eye, along with the selection of tea and coffee displayed on the work surface. Danny turned on the sound system and kept the lights dimmed. Amy couldn't help giggling as he swung her around the dancefloor with her coat and hat on.

When the first dance ended, Amy pulled off her

hat, and her brown hair fell past her shoulders. She hung up her coat on one of the hooks in the entrance hall and insisted that they had one more dance before they tucked into the delicious array of food in the kitchen.

*

Back at the lodge, Seraphina and Justin had eaten their meal and were curled up on the sofa watching family movies eating a box of chocolates. Justin laughed at a young Seraphina bossing Danny around. He heard a man's voice in the background and presumed it must be Seraphina's father before he ran off with the actress.

*

By ten o'clock, Danny and Amy had well and truly danced the night away and tidied all signs of their private party in the village hall. Danny turned the lights out and opened the main door. Their carriage hadn't returned as planned, and a snowstorm was blustering around outside. Danny checked his phone. The driver had sent a text message to advise that the horses wouldn't be venturing out in these weather conditions. He closed the door and looked at Amy.

'We're stranded for the night.'

Amy shivered. 'We can't be. My parents think I'm with Justin. They have no idea I'm with you. What are we going to do?'

Danny called Seraphina. 'Have you looked out of the window recently?'

Seraphina opened the curtains. 'The snow's deep and drifting. Justin had better head off now before it gets worse.'

Amy took the phone from Danny. 'You can't let Justin go home tonight, Seraphina, or I will get in serious trouble. My parents think I've gone out with Justin. Well, I did – but they didn't expect us to split up. This is such a mess!'

Justin took hold of Seraphina's phone. 'Don't panic, Amy. Where are you?'

'The village hall.'

'Well, at least you're safe and inside from the cold. I'll call my parents and say we're stranded. We can meet up in the morning and head back together.'

*

In Seraphina's Lakeside Lodge, Carol Lacey advised the neighbours that Justin and Amy had been stranded and would be staying away for the night. There were winks and smiles all round.

Only Edna Appleby was privy to the truth. From her balcony earlier that evening, she had seen a horse-drawn carriage. Her small pair of theatre binoculars were easy to find. Amy was in that carriage with Danny.

She'd recognise Amy's red bobble hat anywhere – Edna herself had knitted it for Christmas.

It wasn't Edna's place to put the neighbours off the scent of their desire for a budding romance between Justin and Amy. They would find out for themselves soon enough.

Edna was more concerned about Millie. Where had she gone?

12

THE MORNING AFTER

The following morning, the telephone at Greengage Farm didn't stop ringing. Farmer George was in much demand to clear the roads with his snowplough. As far as Farmer George knew, the only people stranded last night were Danny and Amy. He'd taken them to the village hall in his horse-drawn carriage, but he couldn't get them back as planned at ten o'clock. Not wanting to leave a job half-finished, Farmer George cleared a track from the lodges to the village centre as a priority. One of his farmhands followed behind in a Land Rover. Danny and Amy were back at Millie's Lakeside Lodge by nine-thirty.

Justin opened the lodge door. 'So, what did you two get up to last night? Was it nice and cosy in the village hall?'

Amy headed straight to the fire to warm her hands. 'It was freezing after ten o'clock. The heating went off, and we didn't know how to get it back on. We had no other choice but to keep making hot drinks and turning the oven in the kitchen on to get a bit of heat.' Amy yawned. 'I'm soooo tired. We only managed to get a couple of hours sleep on some padded mats we found in a cupboard, didn't we Danny?'

Danny's eyes twinkled. 'You were talking so much; the hall was filled with hot air for most of the night.'

Amy gave Danny a playful thump and Justin raised an eyebrow at Seraphina. It didn't sound like a cold night stranded in the village hall had done much to temper any glimmer of a romance. Justin sensed the opposite was true.

Danny headed for the kitchen. 'Any chance of some pancakes, for us poor lost souls? The things I do to help my sister out. Where did you sleep last night, Justin? You had plenty of bedrooms to choose from?'

Seraphina opened the fridge and took out eggs and milk, before bending down to reach for flour, a bowl, and a whisk. 'Justin insisted on sleeping on the sofa last night. He's becoming accustomed to sofa surfing.'

'I didn't find anything down the back of your sofa though. If your mother hadn't lost her bracelet in our lodge, we wouldn't all be here now watching Seraphina make pancakes. Edna Appleby makes great pancakes, doesn't she, Amy?'

Amy's mouth was watering. 'Not only does she make great pancakes, but she also makes them one-handed. I can't believe she got up so early the day after her accident and insisted on cooking us all breakfast. She's been the least popular neighbour for as long as I can remember. Now she's held up on high as a Fairy Godmother. She'll probably get that tattooed on her ankle and surprise us all even more!'

Seraphina chuckled. 'I had the pleasure of bumping into Edna yesterday morning. I like her.'

Amy helped to set the kitchen table. 'Yesterday morning? Oh, you must have met her when she went into the village to buy materials to make a dinosaur. Only, the shops were shut on a Sunday.'

It was now Justin's turn to giggle, and Seraphina blushed. Amy looked at Danny, who looked at Seraphina. 'OK. I've been rumbled. It was me in the dinosaur costume who fell headfirst into the snow and couldn't get up again.'

Danny burst out laughing. 'It wasn't *my* dinosaur costume, was it?'

Seraphina nodded, and there were fits of giggles all round. Justin was intrigued. 'Why were you in the village on a Sunday when the shops were shut?'

'I was in *my* shop.'

'*Your* shop?'

Danny placed an arm around his sister. 'My sister is accustomed to multi-tasking. Not only does she manage the lodges with our mother, she has her own shop tucked away up a side street in the back of beyond. It's amazing any customers find it.'

Amy was full of interest. 'What do you sell in your shop, Seraphina?'

'Oh, this and that. It's not a very big shop. It used to be my grandfather's; I couldn't bear to have it leave the family when he retired. I spent so much time in there as a young girl. It's nothing more than a hobby really. Anyway, Danny, did you leave the village hall in a tidy state? It's the Tea Dance at four o'clock. Grandma and Grandad won't be too pleased if you've moved a chair or table an inch out of place.'

'Yes. No-one will know it sufficed as our hotel room last night.'

Amy reached for Danny's hand. 'We had fun, didn't we? I must get my dancing ability from my parents. They love a little jig around the place, don't they Justin?'

Justin glanced at a smiling Seraphina and then back

to Amy's hand on top of Danny's. 'Oh, yes, they do. Dora and Jez are always on the dancefloor first at parties. They've even been prancing around in our lodge over the Christmas holidays.' Justin suppressed a giggle. 'I think we should arrange for them to go to the dance this afternoon. Yes, that would be fun!'

Seraphina clasped Danny's other hand. 'Oh, please get them a ticket, Danny. I think Edna and her husband would enjoy it too.' Seraphina looked at Justin. 'Would any more of your neighbours like to go?'

Justin's heart swelled at Seraphina's excitement. He wished he could get all the neighbours to go so that he could spend time alone with this girl who he'd been awake most of the night dreaming about. Justin looked over at Amy, who was nearly falling asleep sitting up. There were still five days of the holiday left. There was time to pace things. Seraphina was only on the other side of the lake. She broke his thoughts. 'How many tickets should Danny get?'

'Oh, just four will do. My parents aren't big dancers, and Sharon and Ryan will need to look after the children. We can't let them go, can we Amy? Or, we'll end up childminding again, and we both need a kip this afternoon.'

Danny helped Amy on with her coat. 'I'll arrange for the tickets to be ready for collection at the door at four o'clock. I hope everyone has a good time. I'll be in touch again before too long.' Danny kissed the top of Amy's head and whispered, 'Thanks for a great time last night.'

On the way back around the lake, Amy and Justin decided to keep their budding romances secret. They didn't want a flare-up between them and their parents about how suited to each other they were, and that the Lacey's and Pritchard's were destined to be joined as a family. They were too tired to think of a way around it. It was best to avoid their disappointment until after the holidays.

13

THE TEA DANCE

Edna and Bill hadn't danced since their wedding, and that was very low-key in the back room of a pub. Edna's parents had long since passed, and Bill came from a small family. Edna was surprised that Bill was keener than her to attempt a waltz around the village hall. He trod on her toes quite a few times, but no-one seemed to notice. They were both too old to care what they looked like and, as Bill spun Edna around, she felt quite giddy.

'That's enough for now, Bill. We should pace ourselves. Let's stop for a bite to eat. Dora and Jez will be cavorting around for hours. There's no need to wait for them. I spotted your favourite egg mayonnaise sandwiches when we did that spin turn near the buffet table.'

A tall, white-haired man with bushy eyebrows and moustache caught Edna's eye. He wore a black pinstripe suit, red polka dot bow-tie, and black and white patent leather shoes. Edna was surprised when he walked over to join her in the buffet queue.

'It's Edna Mayweather, isn't it? You're the spitting image of your mother.'

Edna's knees trembled. 'You knew my mother?'

'My father did; he kept photographs and newspaper articles about her for many years. I remember looking through his scrapbooks as a young boy.'

Edna rubbed her forehead and blamed her dizziness on Bill's power and strength at throwing her around the dancefloor.

'What a small world it is. What brings you to Little Marchampton Village Hall?'

'I'm on holiday with my neighbours.'

'Have you been having a good time.'

Edna thought of her "Fairy Godmother" duties. 'Yes, thank you. I'm having the time of my life!'

The plate of egg mayonnaise sandwiches was becoming depleted, and Edna reached over to grab a couple. When she turned around, tall, white-haired man was gone. She shook her head and tried to gather her thoughts. How weird was that? Maybe dancing didn't suit her after all.

Edna sat down next to Bill, and before she could speak, he squeezed her and gave her a kiss. 'I'm so pleased you insisted we came along on this holiday. I'm really enjoying it. I've just been having a chat with Seraphina's grandmother. She's a lovely lady; her husband was standing behind you in the buffet queue. It's a shame they needed to leave early. She mentioned something about trying to find her daughter.

Dora and Jez flopped down on the chairs opposite. Dora was out of breath. 'What a bonus having a Tea Dance. We should start something up like this back home. Milford-le-Mont won't know what's hit it. Maybe Amy could get us the use of the school hall? Talking of Amy, has anyone heard how she got on with Justin last night? We're only the parents so we'll be the last to know.'

Bill winked. 'They both looked like they needed a good sleep. I've never seen Amy with bags under her eyes like that before. Justin's looked a bit washed up all holiday, but I've put that down to him sleeping on the couch.'

Jez jumped up. 'A quickstep! Come along, Edna, Dora can't keep up with me. Show me your moves.'

Before she could refuse, Edna was whisked onto the dancefloor again. She'd never tell Bill, but Jez was a much better dancer. He held her in his arms and carried her around as if she were a rag doll; her toes just skimmed across the floor. She didn't feel dizzy dancing with Jez who appeared to have an ulterior motive for getting her on her own.

'If I tell you something in private, will you promise not to tell Dora or Carol?' Edna nodded. 'I'm a bit worried about Don. He's been making too many wooden boats for my liking.'

Edna stared at Jez. 'Why on earth would you be worried about that?'

'Well, he used to make one a month, at best. His job in the factory took up most of his time. Over the last few weeks, whenever I've come home early, his car has been parked around the corner.'

'Why would he park his car around the corner?'

'If he didn't want the neighbours to know he'd lost his job.'

Edna gasped. 'Now you come to mention it, the shutters on his shed windows have been closed during the day, and he only used to close them at night. Oh, my goodness, I'd be surprised if Carol knows, she wouldn't have been able to keep something like that secret.'

Jez sighed. 'Well, Carol's been working all hours at the charity shop. She'd never notice if Don were at home during the day. What are we going to do, Edna? I would hate to think that Don's suffering in silence.'

Edna's head was spinning. She'd always avoided Don as she feared he knew her secret. Now that her past was out in the open with Bill, she no longer lived in fear of anyone. Edna had even come to like Don over the Christmas holidays. Surely she'd have a bad feeling if he were in trauma? Jez walked Edna back to their table. 'Any ideas of what we should do?'

Edna looked Jez straight in the eyes. 'We do nothing. I don't have a bad feeling about Don. We just need to mind our own business.'

Jez gulped. That wasn't the reaction he would have expected from Edna. Still, Edna had changed this holiday; she was becoming likeable. Jez hoped her "feelings" were accurate – he'd hate to find out his best friend was in trouble.

As the foursome retrieved their coats from the pegs in the hallway, Edna caught sight of Amy's red bobble hat. She looked over her shoulder then shoved it into her pocket. So, Amy and Danny's romantic ride in a horse-drawn carriage had brought them here last night. Amy wouldn't have gone outside in that snowstorm without her hat. That meant Justin had spent the night alone with Seraphina in Millie's

Lakeside Lodge and Amy had enjoyed a cosy encounter with Danny in the village hall.

Edna smiled to herself all the way back home. She had nothing but good feelings about everything. She also knew it wouldn't be long before she encountered the tall, white-haired man again.

14

TIME TO CLEAR THE AIR

Over breakfast the next morning, Edna was keen to overhear Amy telling her parents that Seraphina had a shop in the village. Carol stared at Justin who's cheeks turned pink every time Seraphina's name was mentioned. She hoped he wasn't playing Amy around. She couldn't deal with a fall out with Dora and Jez. Maybe it wasn't such a good thing trying to push Amy and Justin together.

Jack sat next to Edna, and the young boy's eyes lit up when she discretely put her sausage onto his plate. He knelt on his chair and whispered in her ear, 'Thank you, Mrs Appleby. I have another wish; shall I tell you now or later?'

Edna sighed; she was straining to hear what Amy

was saying down the other end of the table. 'Tell me later, dear. Now sit down and eat your breakfast.'

Dora wanted to know how Amy knew so much about Seraphina. 'Oh, Justin and I have bumped into her when we're out and about.'

Jez noticed Amy lower her eyes. Seraphina was a good-looking girl, was Justin fooling around with her as well as his daughter? He narrowed his eyes to stare at Justin, who felt the heat of anger heading his way.

Edna tried to diffuse the awkward atmosphere. 'Amy, did I hear you saying that Seraphina has a shop? What does she sell? Where is it?'

Amy was grateful for Edna's interjection. 'Apparently, it's up a side street somewhere in the village. She says it used to be her grandfather's shop and when he retired she couldn't bear for it to leave the family. She seems very attached to it.'

Edna's heart was racing. The shop used to belong to tall, white-haired man whose father knew her mother. Edna could visualise what the shop would look like – what services it would sell.

Jack's patience was running out. 'Pleeease, Mrs Appleby. I need to make a wish!' The room fell silent, apart from a few stifled sniggers. Jack took his chance. 'I want to wish for Father Christmas to visit us in his sleigh. He came to visit us last year, and Daddy promised he'd come this year too, but he didn't.'

Sharon put her hands over her eyes and Ryan tried to help Edna out. 'That's right, Jack. Father Christmas did come to visit us again this year, but you didn't see him this time because the day didn't go to plan. Lottie fell in the lake, remember.'

Jack huffed. 'And Mrs Appleby fell down the stairs.'

Ryan smiled at Edna. 'I'm sure your Fairy Godmother can arrange a personal visit from Father Christmas for you and Lottie later on today.'

Edna took comfort from Ryan's knowing stare. 'I'll do my best, Jack. Just leave it with me.'

Jack jumped up and skipped around the room in delight – he was soon joined by Lottie.

Ryan whispered to Edna, 'I have a costume. You don't have to do anything.'

Amy had an idea and joined in the conspiracy. 'I may be able to provide a sleigh of sorts. I know someone who can help.'

Edna was grateful the neighbours were distracted. There was something she needed to do. She looked around for Bill, who had followed Jez and Justin into the games room. That was convenient; once the men went in there they would be gone for hours. She needed a lift into the village though, and the only person available to take her was Don, who had just been outside to bring in more logs for the fire.

Don was pleased that Edna wasn't chatty during the short drive. His mind was on other things; the last thing he needed was a nosey neighbour. Edna jumped out of the car outside the pub and said she'd find her own way home. The fact was, she didn't know how long she would be. Walking home from the village shouldn't be too tiresome, the snow on the roads had been cleared.

It was so early in the morning that no-one was around. Edna didn't know where to start her search for Seraphina's shop. As she walked around the village green, she noticed that most of the curtains were still drawn. The neighbours had been used to getting up at seven during the holidays in line with Jack and Lottie's boisterous start to the day. It was only just before nine now and, at last, Edna heard the pub door open and saw the landlady appear outside with a cleaning bucket. Edna approached her. 'I am not local to here, and I am trying to find Seraphina's shop. Could you please point me in the right direction?'

The landlady gave Edna a strange look then pointed across the village green to a narrow opening that led up a hill. 'If you follow that path, you'll find it.'

Edna headed back around the green and stood at

the foot of the narrow pathway. It looked like quite a climb up the hill, and she wondered if she'd taken on too much. Apart from the bitter cold, her hip was still painful from falling down the stairs. Edna suddenly felt very old. Until now, this holiday had given her a new lease of life. But, however much she hated to admit it, a seventy-five-year-old with a dodgy hip and sore wrist shouldn't be out in the cold on her own attempting to climb a steep, slippery slope at this time in the morning in the middle of winter.

*

Back at the lodge, Bill and Ryan held onto Jez to stop him from punching Justin. 'You've been messing around with Amy, haven't you?'

Justin held his hands up. 'I don't know what you mean.'

'You keep going off with her so that you can bump into that blonde girl. I know what you're like, Justin Lacey, you move from one girl to another without so much as the blink of an eye.'

Don stormed into the games room. 'What's going on here then?'

Carol and Dora shut the kitchen door and held their breath. This fight had been brewing since breakfast. Sharon took the children upstairs to play in their bedroom.

Jez was turning red in the face. 'What's going on, Don, is that your son has led us all to believe he's interested in Amy when that couldn't be further from the truth.'

It was now Don's turn to launch an attack. 'Don't you go throwing rocks at my family. Justin's done nothing wrong; he's as honest as they come.'

Jez's judgement was clouded with anger, and he let rip at his best friend. 'As honest as his father, eh, Don? Does Carol know you've not been going to work these past few weeks? And that you've been hiding in your shed?'

Carol and Dora entered the games room just as Don threw a punch at Jez.

*

Edna was nearing the top of the hill when the door to a small thatched cottage opened and tall, white-haired man stepped out. 'Oh, my goodness, woman. What do you think you're doing? You're blue in the face.' He strode down the garden path and grabbed hold of Edna by her shoulders. 'Come into the cottage. I'll make you a cup of tea. Flissy has gone to the paddock to feed the horses. My name's Raymondo, sorry I didn't introduce myself yesterday, but we've been in a bit of a dilemma as our daughter's gone missing.'

*

Through narrowed eyes, Dora stood back and watched the blood streaming from Jez's lip, which she felt was suitable punishment. She held onto Carol who had turned as white as a sheet. Bill rushed over and placed a chair behind her. Amy had been listening to her father's outburst at Justin and Don from the hallway – she cringed with embarrassment.

All eyes were on Don. 'This wasn't the way I wanted you to find out, Carol. I was made redundant at the factory four weeks ago. They gave me a golden handshake; enough money for us to retire. I didn't know whether to feel happy or sad. I've worked in that factory for over forty years. I'm not ready to retire.'

Carol didn't know whether to laugh or cry, and Justin knelt next to his mother's chair holding her hand. Don continued, 'Anyway, I had an idea that would give us the best of both worlds. I'm going to turn my boat building hobby into a business. I've been working around the clock designing new boats, and I now have a provisional order to supply them to a chain of gift shops on the south coast. I've been really busy, Carol, just the way I like to be. I was waiting for the confirmation to come through after the holidays before giving you the news.'

Jez held out his hand to shake Don's. 'Sorry, mate.'

Don smiled. 'I've wanted to give you a thick lip on

several occasions over the years. I think we're quits now. You can buy me a pint in the pub later.'

Amy took that as her cue to own up about things. She walked into the room and dragged Justin up off his knees. 'Just to make things clear, Justin and I are the best of friends, but we will never be anything else. We're both free agents. If Justin gets a chance with Seraphina, then I'll be delighted. Just think of all those discounted holidays we'll get in these lovely lodges.'

Justin coughed and nodded at Amy, who turned crimson. 'Well, if we're all owning up to things, I should let you know that I find Doctor Danny quite dishy. But enough of that. My main news is top secret and won't be officially announced until the New Year.' A sea of expectant faces focused on Amy. 'When we get back to Milford-le-Mont, I've been promoted to Head Teacher at the primary school.'

Ryan punched the air. 'Just wait until Sharon hears about this. The parents' petition worked – old Dessie's got the sack.'

Sharon walked into the room with the children. 'Did I just hear that right? Amy's going to be Lottie and Jack's Head Teacher?'

Amy nodded, and everyone clapped and cheered.

Dora let out a sigh of relief. It was always good to have a clear the air discussion. 'I don't know about the rest of you, but I think we should have a party. We need to celebrate Don and Amy's new jobs. Why don't we plan one for New Year's Eve? We could invite Seraphina and Danny too.'

More cheers and Bill looked around the room. 'Where's Edna?'

15

SERAPHINA'S SANCTUARY

Holding onto her teacup, Edna began to thaw out. She'd never felt so cold in her life. Apart from her teeth chattering, her feet were so numb that she had no idea how she'd climbed the hill. Raymondo threw some logs onto his open fire, and the crackling noise was the best sound Edna had ever heard. She leant forward to feel the warmth on her face.

'You were lucky there. If I hadn't seen you through the window, you'd have frozen on the spot. Instead of a snowman, there would have been a frozen Edna Mayweather standing outside Seraphina's shop.'

Raymondo chuckled, and Edna looked out of the window. Directly over the road stood a small house with the name "Seraphina's Sanctuary" swinging from a lamp-post outside. 'That's Seraphina's shop?'

'It certainly is. It used to be mine. I was going to sell it when I retired last year, but Seraphina was having none of it. She changed the name, but everything else is the same as I left it.'

Edna could picture an array of crystal balls, tarot cards, and incense sticks. 'May I ask how your father knew my mother?'

'Oh, it's a charming story. Duke Dickie Dreamweaver met Mystic Marigold Mayweather when they both starred in pantomime in London in their late teens. They had such fun that Christmas that, the following summer, they ran off to Brighton to work as clairvoyants on the pier. They did very well without a psychic bone in either of their bodies – they were actors.'

Edna gasped, and her throat felt dry. 'Are you telling me my mother wasn't psychic?'

Raymondo laughed. 'She most certainly was not. You don't believe in that sort of thing, do you?'

'Well . . . I believe in intuition. Some people have gut feelings about things.'

'I put it down to luck and judgement. Your mother brought some luck to Dickie. I remember reading about that.'

'What did she do?'

'She left the fun of Brighton pier the week before my father. On his last night telling fortunes, she telephoned the local fire station and asked them to look out for smoke on the pier. Within an hour, the candyfloss stall next to Dickie's Cryptic Cavern exploded. Having been tipped off by Marigold, the fire brigade was already on the scene. Dickie escaped with a burnt wig and minor smoke inhalation.'

'Oh, my goodness!'

'Stroke of luck, don't you think? Marigold's career as a psychic took off after that. Dickie returned to acting, but he always kept in touch with your mother. He was devastated that she died so young.'

Edna's phone rang. It was Bill. 'Are you all right? Where are you? Don said he dropped you off by the pub over two hours ago.'

'I'm fine, Bill. I'm nearly done here. Would you mind picking me up outside the pub in half an hour?'

'Of course. It's all been kicking off here this morning. I've got lots to update you on.'

'I can't wait to hear, Bill. Make sure you don't forget anything. See you soon.'

Edna looked at Raymondo. 'That was my husband. Thank you for your hospitality.'

Raymondo jumped up. 'You didn't say why you climbed up the hill this morning. What were you looking for?'

Edna blushed. 'I was intrigued to see Seraphina's shop.'

Raymondo reached for a bunch of keys. 'Well, I would be most disappointed if you had a wasted journey. Let me show you inside.'

*

Edna's eyes widened at the sight before her. The shop wasn't as she'd expected – her heart leapt at the vast selection of toys. Raymondo sensed her delight. 'It is rather special, isn't it? I didn't follow my father into acting; I much preferred collecting toys. Seraphina has a website now, and most of her sales come from there. The shop isn't open every day as it's a bit out in the sticks up this hill. Only the locals know it's here.'

Edna's eyes sparkled. 'Oh, I can see why Seraphina loves this shop.'

'She was never out of it when she was young. She must have played with every toy in here. Still, it was a good distraction for her when her parents broke up. She took that very hard. Millie's husband ran off with an actress when Seraphina was just three years' old. Flissy and I blame ourselves for that.'

'Why?'

'Because we didn't approve of Millie's first love. We thought she could do better – we even chose someone for her. As it turned out, she's lived a very lonely life. She's never been interested in another man, and now she's gone missing.'

Edna frowned. 'I thought your daughter had gone on holiday until the New Year. I wouldn't call that missing.'

Raymondo stroked the mane of a rocking horse and kept his eyes to the floor. 'Millie never goes away. I can't remember the last time she had a holiday. She's far too busy. We've tried calling, but her phone is switched off.'

Edna didn't have a bad feeling about Millie. Seraphina and Danny didn't seem concerned about her either. Edna now had another event on her mind. 'How would you like to brighten the lives of two young children?' Raymondo raised his eyebrows and Edna continued, 'With the help of my neighbours we're arranging a little belated Father Christmas trip this afternoon.'

Edna reached into her purse and gave Raymondo a twenty-pound-note. 'If I arrange for Father

Christmas to bring the children to Seraphina's shop, would you be able to supervise them spending ten pounds each on a little memento?'

Raymondo grinned and reached for a pen and paper. 'It would be my pleasure. Here's my number. Call me when Santa's on his way, and I'll unlock the shop.'

16

SLEIGH RIDE

Edna was back at the lodge before lunch. As soon as Amy saw her, she dragged her into her ground floor bedroom. 'This is going to be so exciting, Edna! Danny's arranged for Farmer George to decorate his horse-drawn carriage like a sleigh, with fairy lights and everything! He'll drive it round to the front of the lodge to pick up Sharon, Ryan, Jack, and Lottie at five o'clock when it's dark.'

Edna nodded. 'Good, good. Who's going to wear Ryan's costume?'

'Farmer George, of course, that way Santa will be driving the sleigh.'

Edna nodded again. 'What about presents for the children?'

Amy's shoulders slumped. 'They won't be expecting more presents, will they?'

Edna suppressed a smile. 'I wouldn't want to take any chances. I suggest Danny asks Farmer George to take the children to Seraphina's shop. I was in there this morning. A real treasure trove of toys it is. If they leave here at five, they should be there by five-thirty. I'll make the arrangements from there. You just need to get them to the shop.'

Amy hugged Edna. 'If I'd known you were a Fairy Godmother I'd have made good use of you when I was younger.'

Edna blinked away a tear. 'Go away with you! We should head into the dining room for lunch; it's one o'clock, and I'm ravenous.'

*

Five o'clock couldn't come quick enough for the neighbours. They were all in on the secret except little Lottie and Jack who were excited because their parents were getting them dressed up to go out in the cold so late in the day. Sharon reached for her hat and scarf. 'Go and wait by the front door with Daddy. I'll be with you in a minute.'

Jack looked up at Ryan with wide eyes. 'Where are we going, Daddy? It's dark outside.'

Lottie grabbed her brother's hand. 'I don't like the dark.'

Jack lifted his hat away from his ears. 'What's that noise?'

Sharon pulled her gloves on. 'Go on, Ryan. Open the door, let's see what's outside.'

The Cassidy's stepped out onto the snow-covered lawn to the sight of Father Christmas heading in their direction, driving a sleigh pulled by two white horses. Lottie's mouth fell open, and Jack turned to look through the lounge window into the lodge. The neighbours were lined up smiling, but there was only one neighbour Jack wanted to see. There she was standing in the middle of the group, clapping her hands. Edna stared at Jack, and Jack stared back before mouthing the words: 'Thank you!'

Ryan opened the carriage door for Sharon and the children to climb in. He then joined them and shut the door. Father Christmas made an announcement: 'Yo, ho, ho. It's off we go. Through the snow to a place I know.'

The horses set off at a canter, the sleigh bells jingled, the fairy lights twinkled, and Lottie looked up at Sharon. 'I love Mrs Appleby.'

The sleigh made its way into the village, it did three circles of the village green, then stopped at the foot of a hill which was only accessible through a narrow walkway. Father Christmas jumped off his elevated seat at the front and tied the horses to a lamp-post. 'Follow me off up the hill, don't fall down like Jack and Jill.'

Sharon snorted, and Ryan hugged her. Jack and Lottie walked hand in hand behind Father Christmas, and Sharon and Ryan followed up at the rear. It was quite a climb in the dark, but everyone was in safe hands as Father Christmas led the way with a heavy-duty torch. After a five-minute ascent, the narrow path opened up to reveal a thatched cottage on the right, with curtains open, lights blazing and a tiny white-haired lady peering through the window waving. On the left was a small house with a lamp-post outside and a name swinging from it: "Seraphina's Sanctuary".

As far as the children were concerned, they had made it to the North Pole. That was Father Christmas's house on the right as his wife was waving through the window and they were about to be taken into a magical workshop full of little elves. They weren't disappointed to see just one elf. He was probably the chief elf as he was very tall and very old. They were definitely in Santa's Grotto though as there were lots of really special toys.

Lottie pulled on the hem of Santa's fur-trimmed jacket. 'Ho, ho, ho. What can I do for you, my dear?'

Lottie's eyes shone brighter than Farmer George had ever seen. 'Please tell me your real name. Are you Father Christmas or Santa?'

Farmer George patted his huge stomach then twisted his white moustache. 'I am both, my dear. I travel the world and get called all sorts of different names. I am also known as Saint Nicholas.'

The chief elf stood up and towered over the children who shivered in his shadow. Farmer George wondered how Raymondo had got hold of an elf outfit at such short notice then remembered that Flissy was good with a sewing machine. The elf didn't look so scary when he smiled, and he was even less scary when he made his announcement: 'Santa has brought you both here today to choose a present. You can choose one present each, anything you like. Take your time looking around and if you want to know how anything works then just ask me.'

Ryan whispered to Sharon. 'We'll be here for hours.'

They didn't have to wait for long. Just five minutes later, the children had chosen their presents; Jack wanted the rocking horse and Lottie clung onto a small wooden peg doll. Sharon's cheeks flushed. 'You can't have the horse, Jack. You were supposed to choose something small.'

Jack shook his head. 'The chief elf said we could choose anything we liked.'

Ryan reached for his wallet and whispered to the elf, who also shook his head. Raymondo stared at Farmer George who took that as a signal that the job was done. 'Come along children we need to get Prancer back down the hill. We should be able to fit him in the sleigh.'

Jack hugged the horse's neck. 'I'll take care of you, Prancer. You're my best friend now.'

It was six-forty-five before the neighbours heard the sleigh bells. Edna was shocked to see the Cassidy's emerging from the carriage with a rocking horse. Even she knew that twenty-pounds wouldn't cover the cost of that. She glared at Ryan, who whispered in her ear, 'I tried to pay for it, but the elf wouldn't let me.'

Edna raised her eyebrows. 'The elf?'

'Some tall, white-haired man in the shop.'

Edna was straight on the phone to Raymondo. 'I'm not listening to you, Edna Mayweather. I'm just delighted to have brought some happiness to a young boy. Let's just call it quits – your mother saved my father's life, remember?'

Raymondo ended the call, and Edna muttered, 'How rude.'

Justin helped Ryan carry the rocking horse into the lounge. Ryan reached into his pocket and pulled out a silver bracelet before rushing to the window. 'Oh, drat! Father Christmas has gone, and I found this in his sleigh. I sat on it to be precise.'

Edna jumped up and took the bracelet from Ryan. She glanced at it before putting it into her handbag. 'I know who this belongs to. I'll return it tomorrow.'

17

GREENGAGE FARM

It was the day before New Year's Eve, and Dora and Carol were in the kitchen writing a shopping list for tomorrow night's party. The men were in the games room, and the children were playing happily in the lounge with their new toys. That just left Edna and Amy.

Edna knocked on Amy's bedroom door. 'It's me, Edna. Do you fancy going for a walk?'

Amy opened the door. 'Well, I don't have anything planned.'

Edna smiled. 'Danny working today, is he?' Amy nodded, and Edna continued, 'Do you know the way to the farm? I need to return something to Farmer George.'

Amy confirmed that she did, then grabbed her coat and scarf but couldn't find her hat. Edna reached into her pocket. 'Are you looking for this? Don't forget your gloves.'

Justin heard the sound of footsteps in the hallway and peered out of the games room. 'Where are you two going?'

Amy looked over her shoulder and winked. 'We're on a mission to find the farm. Edna wants to see Santa.'

Justin handed his pool cue to Don. 'Can you take over for me, Dad? I'm off out for a walk. Wait for me, Amy. I'll come with you.'

The narrow track to the farm was easy to find in the daylight. Amy led the way, her thoughts wandering back to the other night when Danny had brought her down here and the excitement she felt when he told her she should try good guys, instead of bad ones. She could picture the carriage and horses waiting at the end of the track and felt the softness of the fleece blanket Danny had wrapped around their legs.

Justin nudged Edna and nodded towards Amy at the front. 'Quiet, isn't she? Seems to know where she's going, though.'

It felt like an eternity in the cold, but the track eventually widened and brought the sight of the farm with it. Amy turned around. 'Well, I got you here. Edna can lead the way to Santa. He might be mucking out the horses or milking a few cows.' Justin chuckled, and Edna headed straight for the main house. There was a sign above the doorbell: "Greengage Farm". Edna rang the bell – there was no answer.

With snow on the ground and the prospect of more to come, Edna headed for a barn. The door was shut, and the lights were on. Edna peered through a window then tapped on it. The door opened to the sight of Danny wearing a visor. Amy caught her breath. 'I thought you were working today?'

Danny lifted his visor. 'I am.'

Farmer George strode though the barn and stood with hands on hips as he surveyed the stunned faces. 'Danny's not just a doctor, you know. He's quite a gifted craftsman.'

Amy raised her eyebrows and Danny blushed before holding out his hand to reveal a silver bracelet with the name "Amy" carved into the band. 'You weren't supposed to see this until it's finished.'

Amy clasped a hand over her mouth, and Justin filled the silence. 'So, you made Seraphina's and Millie's bracelets too. I would never have guessed that Doctor Danny was so creative.'

Edna felt the coolness of the bracelet in her pocket. The revelation that Danny was the craftsman had thrown her off track. If Farmer George had been making bracelets, then her suspicions would have been spot on.

Farmer George smiled at Edna. 'So, what can we do for you on this fine day?'

Edna opened her mouth, but no words came out. Justin's mind was spinning; he'd heard the farmer's distinctive deep voice before – he was sure of it. He just couldn't remember where. Amy nudged Edna, who blurted out the first thing that came to mind. 'We were just passing. You're obviously busy; we'll leave you to it.' Edna turned around, and an embarrassed Amy and Justin followed.

The trio were half-way back up the narrow track when Justin remembered where he'd heard the farmer's voice. 'Got it!'

Edna and Amy stopped walking and stared at Justin. 'This is really weird, but I'm sure I'm right. I was watching family movies with Seraphina the other night, and a man's voice kept popping up in the background; I think it was the farmer. He may have been the one filming Millie and her children. There were no other men around. Seraphina said her father left home when she was three.'

Edna closed her eyes, hallelujah! Her suspicions weren't wrong after all; she took an about-turn. 'You two should head back to the lodge; there's more snow on the way. I've just remembered why I needed to see Farmer George. I'll pop back to the farm – I won't be long.'

Edna peered through the barn window. Farmer George was leaning over Danny while he worked on Amy's bracelet. Edna removed the bracelet from her pocket and read the inscription inside the band: "We'll be together one day. I promise." Danny wouldn't engrave that message to his mother – but Farmer George would!

Farmer George looked up to see Edna. He left Danny at the workbench and walked outside, closing the barn door behind him. 'Don't tell me you're lost.'

Edna smiled up at him. 'I'm not lost, but someone is, and I think I've found her. Millie's in the farmhouse, isn't she?'

Farmer George's mouth fell open, and Edna handed him the bracelet. 'I've pieced most of it together. Millie was your first love, and you were hers. Her parents thought she could do better than you and she married that millionaire who left her for an actress. You've been in the background ever since, helping Millie and her children. What I can't work out is, why is it only now that Millie's been brave enough to do a runner and move in with you?'

Farmer George nodded towards the barn. 'It was Danny. We've always been close. He knows I love Millie.'

Edna's eyes widened. 'Go on.'

'Well, Danny said that Millie had spent too long trying to please her parents and he packed her bag and gave it to me. I picked her up in the horse-drawn carriage while the youngsters were in the pub at lunchtime on Boxing Day. What surprised me most was that Millie didn't complain at all. She just switched her phone off and said she'd deal with her parents in the New Year. Danny covered for her, and the rest is history.'

Edna smiled up at George. 'How delightful!'

A huge flake of snow fell on Farmer George's head, and Edna pulled her coat around her. Farmer George looked to the sky. 'That pathway will soon be blocked if the snow keeps falling as thick as this. I'll drive you home in the Land Rover.'

18

NEW YEAR'S EVE MORNING

C arol was in a flap. There were already twelve neighbours to cater for, and tonight there would be two guests: Seraphina and Danny. Justin ate a cocktail sausage straight from the oven. Carol slapped his hand. He sensed his mother's anxiety. 'Don't panic, Mum. You're only doing a buffet.'

'I thought Dora would be in here helping me by now.'

'She wanted Jez to drive her into the village to get a few last-minute bits.'

'What bits? We went shopping yesterday. 'Where's Sharon, can't she help make some cheese straws?'

'She's gone for a walk with Ryan and the children.'

The doorbell rang, and Carol stared at Justin. 'Well, aren't you going to answer that? I can't do everything.'

Justin opened the front door to the sight of a middle-aged man with neatly-styled dark brown hair and glasses. He wore a suit and carried a large bouquet of red roses. 'I've come to see Amy.'

Justin let the man into the lounge and knocked on Amy's bedroom door. 'There's someone here to see you.'

Amy jumped off her bed, and her heart leapt at the thought of Danny arriving with her bracelet. She brushed her hair, put on some lip gloss, and glided down the hall to be met by Justin. 'I've put him in the lounge.'

Amy's smile shone as she put her head around the door. It soon diminished when she saw her guest. She stepped into the lounge and shut the door behind her. 'What are you doing here?'

Desmond stood up and tried to hand the bouquet to Amy. 'I've left her. I said I would.' Desmond coughed. 'I've also left my job. So, it's New Year and a new start for us. As I'm a man of honour, I couldn't wait to see your reaction when you knew I'd kept my promise. I thought we could see in the New Year together then when we get back, I'll move into your apartment.'

Amy took hold of the roses and swiped them back and forth against Desmond as if they were a foil in a bout of fencing. Sharon and Ryan peered through the lounge window to witness Amy's rebuffed admirer ducking and diving to avoid the onslaught.

When they saw Amy grab his arm and lead him back into the hall, they hid around the back of the lodge where the children were attempting to build a snow castle. They heard the front door slam and peered down the lane to see the back of Milford-le-Mont's former Head Teacher disappear into the distance. Sharon's eyes were on stalks, and Ryan pressed a finger to his lips. 'We didn't see that. Dora and Jez would be mortified if they knew old Dessie boy had eyes for their daughter.'

Dora and Jez had other concerns. After finishing their last-minute shopping, they popped into the pub. They couldn't believe their eyes when they saw Rachel sitting by the fire. Dora called over to her, 'Rachel! What are you doing here?'

Rachel looked up. 'Oh, hello, Dora. I'm staying above the pub tonight. I've just checked in. You could say I'm on a mission. I'm here to win Justin back. I thought New Year's Eve was as good a time as any for him to make a commitment to me. He'll be devastated I dumped him before Christmas. It'll be a case of "absence makes the heart grow fonder" just you wait and see.'

Justin followed Desmond down the lane at a discreet distance. He wanted to make sure old Dessie was well and truly out of Amy's life. She deserved so much better than a loser like him. Desmond turned into the pub, and so did Justin.

Desmond went straight to the bar. 'Do you have any rooms available for tonight?'

The barman shook his head. 'Sorry, you're out of luck. The young lady by the fire has just taken the last one.'

Justin turned to look at the young lady. He recognised her straight away, and he stormed over. 'Rachel! What are you doing here?'

Rachel gazed up at Justin with sparkling eyes. 'I'm here to win you back, Justin. You must be missing me.'

Justin pulled at his hair and let out a strangled cry. 'You shouldn't have come here. I'm not missing you – I'm in love with somebody else.'

Justin stepped back in surprise at his own words. He turned around to walk out of the pub and noticed Farmer George sitting behind the door. He tipped his cap to Justin and winked. Dora and Jez nudged each other and sipped their coffees; that was Rachel and

Justin well and truly over. Now, why had Amy's boss suddenly appeared from nowhere?

Desmond sat down next to a distraught Rachel. 'May I buy you a drink? You can do better than a boy like him. If you're at a bit of a loss now on New Year's Eve then why don't I buy you lunch?'

Dora and Jez finished their drinks and made a quick getaway. They had so much news to pass on to the neighbours. When they reached the lodge, Dora headed straight for the kitchen. 'You'll never guess what, Carol; Rachel's in the pub down the road and Justin well and truly told her where to go. On top of that, Amy's old boss at the school turned up too. I've no idea what he's doing up here.'

Amy was tired of the knowing glances she had been receiving from Sharon and Ryan since Desmond's departure. They must have seen him come to the lodge. She tried her best to diffuse the situation while most of the neighbours were in earshot. 'Desmond came here for a handover. New Year, new start, that kind of thing. It's best we don't carry things over until the school starts back next week. We're all sorted now. It was very good of him to come all this way.'

Sharon raised an eyebrow at Ryan and decided it was best to leave things at that. Amy was going to make a brilliant Head Teacher for Lottie and Jack. From what Dora told Sharon, old Dessie boy was all over Rachel in the pub. Amy had done well to fend off his advances.

After Dora's exciting morning, she felt guilty about not helping Carol prepare for tonight's party. 'Why don't you take the afternoon off, Carol? You go and glam up, and I'll take up the reins. I'll rope the men into putting up the decorations. It should be a good do tonight. I'm looking forward to it.'

19

NEW YEAR'S EVE PARTY

By the time Seraphina and Danny arrived, the neighbours had already sampled the "Party Punch". Don was well-known for mixing a few cocktails at summer barbeques, so he was given the job of supervising a make-shift bar in the kitchen.

Seraphina handed a platter of canapés to Carol. 'We didn't want to come empty-handed, so Danny's been helping me make these this afternoon.'

Carol was delighted. 'How thoughtful! Why don't you go through to the lounge? Just make yourselves at home.'

As it was a special occasion, the children were allowed to stay up for as long as they wanted. They had energy in abundance – fuelled by the odd sweet from

Edna. Jack sat astride his rocking horse to greet their guests. Seraphina raised her eyebrows at Danny then headed straight for the horse. She stroked its mane as she smiled at Jack. 'His name's Prancer, you know.'

Jack held his shoulders back and clutched the reins. 'I know. Santa told me.'

Danny stood next to the fire with his arm around Amy. 'Trust Grandad to finally get rid of Prancer. He took offence to him when George made him for me when I was little. He's never liked that horse.'

Edna listened to Danny's words from her seat on the end of the sofa. Raymondo may be charming on the outside, but he wasn't kind on the inside. He'd stopped Millie marrying George, he'd given away a much-treasured rocking horse that should have stayed within his family, and he'd made fun of Marigold Mayweather's psychic abilities. In Edna's eyes, Raymondo's actions were unforgivable.

Amy rested her head on Danny's shoulder. 'How's my bracelet coming along?'

Danny blushed. 'It's nearly finished. I hope you like it.'

'I love it already.'

'I can't believe you'll be leaving the day after tomorrow.'

'I know. It doesn't seem fair. Why has it taken me so long to realise that good guys are the best?'

Dora clapped her hands to gain everyone's attention, and Jez emerged from the kitchen with a tray of champagne-filled glasses. Dora commenced an impromptu speech. 'Sorry about the mismatch of glasses, but champagne tastes the same out of whatever container it's served in. I've seen footballers on the TV drink it out of big silver cups, and racing drivers even spray it around everywhere and drink it straight from the bottle.'

Jez surveyed the sea of puzzled faces and decided to take over from his wife. 'On behalf of the neighbours, we would like to congratulate Don on his non-retirement. What a stroke of luck – a golden handshake and a new job to boot! I'm sure you're all as delighted as us about Amy's promotion, and there's just one more person to mention; if it hadn't been for Carol's idea, we wouldn't all be here now having the time of our lives! I would like to propose a toast to Don, Amy and Carol.'

Everyone cheered and clinked glasses, and Justin turned up the music.

*

Millie and George had just finished a cosy dinner-for-two in the farmhouse. Millie's eyes danced with mischievousness. 'I think it's time we come clean, George. We should pay my parents a visit.'

George stood up and reached for his coat. 'Let's go now before you change your mind.'

The Land Rover stood at the foot of the hill as Millie and George made the challenging climb. George carried a torch and Millie clung onto him so that she didn't lose her footing on the icy surface. She felt like a teenager again – taking George to meet her parents. Only this time Millie wasn't going to come away with a bad result, she was determined about that. Too many years had been wasted.

The curtains of the thatched cottage were drawn, and Millie took a deep breath. George stepped forward and shone his torch into the window of Seraphina's shop. 'I don't believe it. He said he'd destroyed it.'

Millie slapped a gloved hand to her mouth while she took in the sight. Her shock soon turned to anger. 'His conscience is pricking, and he's going to come clean with Seraphina. He's got a nerve. All those years Seraphina thought you favoured Danny over her. She was distraught that Christmas, her father had let her down and she believed you had too. No wonder she's never trusted a man.'

The door to the cottage opened, and Raymondo stepped outside. 'Hello, Millie. I was worried about you for a while, but Flissy worked out where you were hiding. I'm too old now to keep interfering in your life. I hope you are happy with the farmer.'

Millie held her head high. 'His name's George, and I am very happy.'

George stepped forward and held out his hand to Raymondo. 'I'm prepared to call a truce under one condition.'

Raymondo rubbed his chin. 'What's that?'

'We take the rocking horse away with us now.'

Raymondo stepped back inside the cottage and returned with a bunch of keys. He unlocked Seraphina's shop. George lifted the horse out of the window display and placed it on the snow outside.

Millie wasn't so quick to forgive her father. 'You will have to own up to Seraphina. She may never forgive you. You do realise how stubborn she is, don't you?'

Raymondo hung his head in shame, and Millie was surprised to see how old he looked. Her dominant, stubborn father had turned into a broken man. Tears welled in her eyes at all the unnecessary years of heartache. 'It's a new year tomorrow, Dad, the best time for a fresh start. Thank you for accepting George into our family.'

Millie hugged her father, and George smiled at him before turning around and carrying the horse down the icy hill.

With Dancer safely in the back of the Land Rover, George and Millie headed straight for Seraphina's Lakeside Lodge. George lifted the horse out of the car and placed it outside the front door before driving Millie home to the farm.

Millie emailed Justin:

Hello Justin

If you open the front door, there is something outside that will delight Seraphina.

Love Millie x

Justin opened the front door, then closed it again. He was taken aback. Why was there a rocking horse on the doorstep, and why wasn't Millie away on holiday? Danny saw Justin scratching his head. 'What's up? You look like you've seen a ghost.'

Justin opened the front door again and showed Danny the horse. Danny raised his eyebrows. 'Oh, my goodness. I knew George wouldn't make just one horse for me. We were staying at our grandparents' house that Christmas – Grandad must have hidden it. He never liked George.' Danny looked at Justin. 'Why has it turned up now?'

Justin shrugged his shoulders. 'I've no idea. Your mother just emailed to let me know it was outside. I thought she was away on holiday.'

Danny's cheeks glowed. 'She's not on holiday – she's moved in with George. Seraphina doesn't know yet.'

Seraphina stepped into the hall. 'What don't I know?'

Danny held the lodge door open to the sight of Dancer. 'Mum's not on holiday. She's moved in with George. George isn't the bad guy you thought he was by treating me differently to you. He made me Prancer, but he made you Dancer too. Dancer just got a bit lost on his way from the North Pole that Christmas, but he's turned up now.'

Seraphina held both hands to her mouth, and her blue eyes glowed. 'Well, you'd best bring Dancer in then. He'll be getting cold outside.'

Seraphina needed time to gather her thoughts. Where had her rocking horse been all these years? Why had it only just turned up now? She was shocked her mother had moved into the farmhouse. Her grandfather had never liked George. No! It couldn't be true. Grandad wouldn't have hidden her horse to make her dislike George too, would he?

Danny read his sister's thoughts. 'I think our

grandfather has some owning up to do. But that's for another day. You're a bit big for Dancer now, you were only three when George made him. What will you do with him now?'

Seraphina turned around to see Ryan carrying Lottie upstairs on his shoulder. She was fast asleep. Seraphina knew what she would do with her rocking horse.

Don rushed into the hall. 'Come along, everyone. It's nearly midnight. Dora's just putting the TV on for Auld Lang Syne.'

At the stroke of midnight, Justin kissed Seraphina, and she felt her heart begin to melt. Her mother moving in with George was a huge testimony to the fact that not all men were bad. When Seraphina thought back to that first Christmas after her father had left, she remembered her grandfather making a big deal of Danny receiving a present from George and not her. After Seraphina's initial disappointment, she knew that George wouldn't be so cruel. Two days later, he came to the lodge and gave her a miniature carved rocking horse that she kept in her pocket. Throughout her childhood, it was her most treasured possession. She'd always had a special bond with George – one that her grandfather couldn't break.

20

NEW YEAR'S DAY

With most of the neighbours having a lie-in, Edna had time to plan her final Fairy Godmother duty of the holiday. Before Seraphina had left in the early hours of the morning, she had asked Edna to give Dancer to Lottie. Edna was humbled by Seraphina's generosity and embarrassed that the neighbours would be returning to Milford-le-Mont with two "free gifts" that would cost a fortune to buy in the shops.

Seraphina wouldn't take "no" for an answer. She said that Prancer and Dancer were meant to be together. Edna had no choice but to carry out Seraphina's wish. She was sure Lottie would be thrilled; it was a fitting bonus for the little girl who had become attached to a tiny peg doll with a three-pounds price tag after her brother had chosen the most expensive item in the shop.

The thud of tiny feet down the stairs did nothing to wake Justin on the sofa. Edna ushered the children into the kitchen. 'What would you both like for breakfast?'

Without their parents in earshot, Jack tried his luck. 'Chocolate cake and ice cream.'

Lottie sat up straight, she knew her brother was chancing his luck, and Mrs Appleby was so nice that she might even grant his request. It would be his fault if he were sick before lunchtime, not Mrs Appleby's. Lottie decided to be good. 'Toast and juice, please.'

Edna reached for a loaf of bread and took a carton of orange juice out of the fridge. 'It's toast and juice for both of you then.' Jack opened his mouth to complain, and Edna continued, 'Lottie used the magic word, and Jack forgot, so Lottie's choice wins.'

Lottie whispered to her brother. 'You didn't say "please".'

While Jack was on the back foot, Edna tried to put in place her cunning plan. 'You must be so pleased, Jack, to be taking Prancer home. All your friends will want to have a go on him, and Lottie's friends too.'

Jack frowned; he hadn't thought about sharing his

rocking horse. Mrs Appleby had a point though – Prancer would be in big demand back home.

Edna continued while the boy's brain was ticking over. 'It's a shame that there weren't two rocking horses then you could have had one each. That way, you wouldn't have to share quite so much.' Edna waited, that should do it. Jack would wish for another rocking horse any second now. He didn't.

Lottie's eyes filled with tears. 'Do you think Prancer will be lonely when we take him all the way home? He'll be leaving all his friends behind.'

Jack stared at his sister. 'He's a rocking horse. He won't have friends.'

Edna smiled at Lottie and willed her on. If Jack wouldn't make a wish, then Lottie would.

Lottie placed her toast back on her plate. 'I wish you hadn't chosen Prancer.'

Edna squirmed inside; this was all going horribly wrong. Jack shot a glance at Edna. 'Don't say that, Lottie, or he'll go away in a puff of smoke. Don't wish for that. I wish he had a friend, but that's never going to happen. Just don't wish for him to go away.'

Edna let out a sigh of relief. She sent a text to Bill.

PLEASE BRING DANCER OUT OF
THE HALL CUPBOARD AND STAND
HIM NEXT TO PRANCER.

Justin stirred when he heard Bill enter the lounge carrying the rocking horse. He sat up on the sofa and squinted at Prancer and Dancer standing next to each other. All excitement would let loose soon – he needed to get dressed. 'Any chance of using your en-suite, Bill?'

'Of course. Edna's in the kitchen. Take as long as you want.'

Don and Carol passed Justin on the stairs. 'Happy New Year, Justin!'

Justin smiled at his parents before bumping into Sharon and Ryan on the landing. Sharon's hair resembled a bird's nest, and Ryan was a dodgy shade of green. Justin was pleased he'd kept his consumption of alcohol to a minimum last night. His focus had been on Seraphina.

With Carol and Don now in the kitchen, Edna was keen for the rest of the neighbours to surface so that her final "Fairy Godmother" duty of the holiday could be witnessed. She didn't have long to wait, Sharon and Ryan were soon followed by Dora, Jez, and Amy.

The children were distracted by their parents' arrival and the promise of more food. Edna left Bill, keeping everyone contained in the kitchen, and went in search of Justin. As she passed the lounge, she looked in to see Prancer and Dancer standing proud, and her heart leapt. She couldn't think of a time when she'd had a happier holiday.

Edna climbed the stairs and knocked on her bedroom door. 'Justin! You need to come downstairs now. The fun's about to start. Don't take too long or you'll miss it.'

Justin emerged from Edna's bedroom, drying his hair with a towel. 'Thanks for the loan of your en-suite. Nice shower gel by the way. I'll buy Mum some next Christmas.'

Justin handed the towel to Edna and made his way down the stairs. Edna went into her bedroom to see what mess Justin had made this time and found a letter folded up on the floor. Edna read it:

Dear Seraphina

It was great meeting you this holiday. Unfortunately, all good things must come to an end. By tomorrow evening I'll be back home with my parents.

It's a shame we live so far apart. Long-distance relationships just don't work.

I'll be busy today helping the neighbours pack their things ready for an early start in the morning. That's why I've written you this letter.

Goodness knows how we're going to get two rocking horses home. We'll need to do a bit of shuffling around in the cars to achieve that.

All the best, Justin.

Edna's heart sank. Justin was going to break it off with Seraphina before things had even started. She'd had higher hopes for Justin than that. Edna heard a low whistle coming from the hallway and knew that was Bill's signal for her to go back downstairs. Edna was annoyed with Justin, but she wouldn't let his shallowness spoil the last day of the holiday.

Jack and Lottie escaped Bill's security duties and ran into the lounge to the sight of two rocking horses.

Lottie's face reddened. 'I didn't wish for two. I wished you hadn't chosen Prancer.'

Jack was aghast. 'Mummy and Daddy are going to be so cross. They were cross with me when I chose one and now I've got two.' He had an idea. 'Help me push one behind the curtains. No-one will know.'

Edna watched the children from the hallway. What on earth were they doing? The doorbell rang, and Edna opened the front door. 'Seraphina! You're up early.'

'I was just wondering if Justin was about.'

Edna glanced down at the letter in her hand. 'I think he's a bit busy today.'

Seraphina noticed her name on the letter. 'Would you like to give that to me?'

Edna handed it over. Seraphina read the letter then strode into the lounge. 'What are you children doing with Dancer? He doesn't like hiding behind curtains.'

Lottie's eyes widened. 'He's called Dancer?'

'Yes. He used to be my rocking horse, and now he's yours, Lottie. It's my biggest wish that he goes home with you so that he can be close to Prancer. They're best friends, you know.'

Lottie hugged Dancer and Jack stared at Edna. She'd done it again; the Fairy Godmother had worked her magic. Jack climbed onto Prancer – his parents couldn't be annoyed if Mrs Appleby had sorted everything out.

Edna touched Seraphina's arm. 'I don't think he means it, dear. It's all very strange.'

Seraphina smiled. 'I know. He's up to something. I'll just have to wait to see what it is.'

Seraphina walked out of the lodge carrying the letter, and the neighbours headed straight from the kitchen to the lounge to witness the children's delight at becoming the proud owners of twin rocking horses.

Edna tapped Justin on his shoulder. 'You dropped a letter in my bedroom. It was addressed to Seraphina. She popped round five minutes ago. I gave it to her.' Edna waited for Justin's reaction.

'Good. That saves me a trip around the lake to post it. Thanks, Edna.'

21

THE FAIRY GODMOTHER'S REWARD

After helping their parents pack away their toys, Jack and Lottie were at a loss with what to do. They rummaged through the sideboard in the lounge and pulled out all the games and jigsaws they could find. Jack huffed. 'These are all too hard.'

Lottie had a suggestion. 'Why don't we make Mrs Appleby a present?'

Jack thought that was a good idea; it was best to keep in the good books of their Fairy Godmother. The trouble was all their crayons and paper were now in the boot of the car. Jack sighed, then came up with an ingenious idea that surprised both of them.

'We should give Mrs Appleby a present from the

neighbours. We don't need to make anything. We just need to collect things. Let's find a box in the kitchen first; then we'll fill it with presents when no-one's looking.'

An empty cereal box was as good a container as any. The children peered out of the lounge window and saw Dora, Jez and Amy loading their car. Finding presents from their bedrooms was the first place to start.

Sharon and Ryan were surprised the children were playing nicely in the lodge. They had no idea why they were walking around with an empty cereal box, but they were pleased they were using their imaginations to devise some sort of a game.

By five o'clock, Jack and Lottie had managed to dodge all the neighbours, fill the box with presents and find Mrs Appleby sitting on the sofa next to the fire. Jack clutched hold of the box, and Lottie spoke: 'This is a present from the neighbours.' Jack handed the box to Edna.

Edna felt inside and pulled out a wet flannel. She'd seen that on Carol's washing line back home. Next came a smelly black sock with a hole in the toe. Jez was wearing that last night. A blue tie followed – that belonged to Bill. Edna folded it neatly and placed it on the sofa next to her.

Lottie frowned. 'We went into every bedroom to find something, but we couldn't get you a present from Justin as he doesn't have a room. He sleeps on the sofa.'

Edna smiled. 'That doesn't matter, dear. You've been very thoughtful, bringing me all these gifts.' Edna planned to give them all back as soon as the children had gone to bed. By process of elimination, there should be two presents left: One from Amy and one from the Cassidy's. Edna reached into the box again and pulled out a chocolate bar. That could have been anyone's. There was just one thing left in the box now, and Edna shook it around so that it rattled. She tipped the box upside down and out fell . . . a positive pregnancy test!

Edna's mouth fell open. 'Where did you find this?'

Jack shrugged his shoulders, and Lottie rubbed her forehead. 'I can't remember. Do you like your present?'

Edna shook her head, then nodded. She was flustered. What should she do now? Either Amy or Sharon was pregnant. With the children back on their rocking horses having a "race" Edna did the most sensible thing. She walked past Dora and Jez's room and threw the black sock through the open door. She ran upstairs and left Carol's flannel outside her room. Bill's tie went straight into Edna's washing bag. That just left the pregnancy test and the chocolate bar. Edna headed for the kitchen, left the chocolate bar on the work surface, and shoved the pregnancy test down the bottom of the bin. The children didn't know what it was, and Edna didn't want to be party to something so private. Out of sight, out of mind, was a good motto. Edna vowed to forget all about that unfortunate incident.

*

Edna couldn't help noticing how quiet Amy was over dinner. She hardly ate anything. At eight o'clock, the doorbell rang, and Amy jumped up from her place at the table to answer it. There were hushed voices in the hall, and Amy didn't return to finish her meal. Edna quizzed Justin. 'Did Amy have a boyfriend before we came away?'

Justin savoured another mouthful of trifle. He spoke with his mouth full which Edna would usually have chastised him for. 'Yep. She dumped him though before Christmas.'

Sharon helped Carol clear the table, and Edna walked down the hallway to the sound of sobbing coming from Amy's room. On passing the kitchen, she saw Sharon pick up the chocolate bar and bite the end off before placing it back on the work surface and loading the dishwasher. Edna sighed; that was the worst possible case scenario. She had a bad feeling coming on and decided to have an early night.

Amy lay on her bed and held the silver bracelet close to her chest. Danny had made it for her. He'd given it to her tonight rather than in the morning as he said he "didn't like goodbyes". Amy read the inscription inside the band over and over again: "Until we meet again."

However hard she tried; Amy couldn't think of a way to make things work with Danny. She was starting her new job as the Head Teacher of Milford-le-Mont Primary next week, and Danny was a doctor who lived over five hours away. She was stupid to have gone along with Justin's half-baked idea of getting to know Seraphina. Everything had been doomed from the start.

Justin knocked on Amy's door. 'Can I come in?' He heard a muffled 'Yes', so he walked in to the sight of Amy with mascara all down her face. He chose not to mention it. 'We're in a bit of a predicament about getting the rocking horses back with us tomorrow. Edna and Bill are going to take one on the back seat of their car, and Mum and Dad said they'll take the other. That leaves me without a lift home unless I join you in the back of your parents' car. I just thought I should let you know so that it's not a shock in the morning.'

Amy blew her nose. 'Whatever.'

Justin took that as her acceptance of the situation and headed into the games room to find Ryan and Bill clinking beer glasses. Justin raised his eyebrows and Ryan summoned him over. 'If I tell you a secret, will you promise to keep it?' Justin nodded. 'I've told Bill as it just sort of slipped out. Sharon's pregnant.'

Justin high-fived Ryan. 'So, you're telling me that if we come here again, we'll not only need an extra bedroom for me, we'll need a cot?'

Ryan's smile lit up the room. 'That about sums it up. Anyway, I'll be heading off upstairs soon. Sharon's gone to bed early – she's whacked.'

With Sharon, Edna and Amy all having early nights. It wasn't long before the rest of the neighbours followed. Justin had the luxury of getting to bed early too. The sofa was available from nine o'clock. He carried his bed linen from the cupboard under the stairs and reflected on the last two weeks. What a whirlwind. Who would have guessed that Christmas with the neighbours would have been so eventful?

22

TIME TO HEAD HOME

If Edna didn't have to get up for the drive home, she would have stayed in bed. She'd had a nagging feeling all last night and couldn't quite put her finger on what was wrong. Bill went downstairs and made her a cup of tea. She hadn't been like this since Christmas Day.

Edna sat up in bed, warming her hands on the cup. 'I've got a bad feeling, Bill. I think that Amy may be pregnant and she's broken things off with the father back home.'

Bill rubbed his chin. 'That would be unfortunate. Sharon's pregnant too, but Ryan has asked me not to tell anyone.'

Edna put the cup on its saucer and jumped out of bed. 'That means Amy's not pregnant.' Edna hugged

Bill and decided to take a quick shower.

After the euphoria of the pregnancy news, Edna was surprised that the nagging feeling wouldn't go away. She sat on the end of her bed and channelled her thoughts. It wasn't long before Edna could predict what was going to happen this morning. She felt relieved. There was no need for her to intervene; everything happened for a reason.

After a quick breakfast of cereal and toast, Don took the bin bags out to the refuse collection area, and the neighbours checked their bedrooms to ensure they hadn't missed packing anything. Dora loaded the dishwasher for the last time, and Carol straightened the cushions in the lounge. Everyone stepped outside together and took one last look at the snow-covered lakeside lodges.

Don placed an arm around Carol's shoulders. 'You did well to find this place. Everyone had a great time.'

Sharon and Ryan strapped Lottie and Jack into their car seats, and Prancer and Dancer stood proudly on the back seats of the Lacey's and Appleby's cars. Amy climbed into her parents' car and waited for Justin.

Lottie remembered something. 'Mrs Appleby!'

Edna could hear the young girl calling her name and wandered over to the Cassidy's car to see what she wanted. Lottie's eyes lit up at the sight of her Fairy Godmother. Lottie held the peg doll out of the car window. 'This is for you, Mrs Appleby. It's a present from me.'

Edna took hold of the doll and swallowed hard. 'Thank you, Lottie. I shall treasure it forever.'

With three of the four cars fully-loaded, the neighbours began to head off on the long journey home. Amy was annoyed that Justin was taking so long to get into the car. The temperature was below freezing; it would take ages for the heater to warm up.

*

In Millie's Lakeside Lodge, Seraphina had awakened with a bad feeling too. She'd been deep in thought over breakfast with Danny. Suddenly her vision became crystal clear. She needed to get out of the lodge as quickly as possible. Jumping up, she grabbed her coat and ran around the lake towards the village.

Danny stood up and closed the door behind her. 'Bye, Sis! Hope you have a good day.'

*

Edna requested Bill to take a slight diversion around the village green. She asked him to park outside the village hall as that would be an excellent viewing point. On the stroke of ten o'clock, Seraphina ran past their car and headed for the hill to her shop.

Edna was satisfied with that. 'Drive on, Bill. Seraphina has everything covered.'

Seraphina commenced the ascent in time to witness her grandfather lose his footing on the slippery slope and slide down the hill in a most undignified manner. Seraphina held onto a railing with her left hand and caught hold of his coat with her right.

Raymondo let out a cry. 'You saved me, Seraphina! I was heading straight for that wall.'

Seraphina helped her grandfather to his feet. 'Why did you hide my rocking horse?'

Raymondo brushed the snow off his coat. 'Because that farmer made it. He was getting far too close to you children. Anyone would have thought he was your father.'

Seraphina sighed. 'Well, you must know by now that your interfering didn't work. George ended up being the only father figure we could count on. All I can say, is that I'm delighted my mother has finally stood up to you, you miserable old man.'

Raymondo gasped. 'You can't call me that! I'm your grandfather.'

Seraphina turned and walked away. She muttered under her breath. 'Oh, yes, I can.' A wry smile touched her lips. It would be good for her grandfather to suffer for a few days; she'd forgive him soon enough. At least she'd saved him a hospital trip.

*

At last! The car door opened, and Justin jumped in. Amy was reading a book. 'Nice of you to finally turn up.'

Dora shot a look at Jez, who raised his eyebrows and looked in his rear-view mirror to witness Amy's reaction.

'That's not very nice. It's taken me a great deal of effort to sort this out.'

Amy's head spun round. 'Danny!'

'That's right. I've swapped places with Justin. I hope you don't mind.'

Amy couldn't get her words out. 'What? How?'

'I've taken a week's leave to consider my future. My manager wants me to go on secondment to a hospital in London. I thought I could hitch a lift down south with you.' Danny smiled at Amy's parents. 'I hope you don't mind, Mr & Mrs Pritchard?'

Dora's cheeks glowed, and she patted her hair. 'Of course not, Danny. Just call us Dora and Jez, you're practically family now.'

*

Seraphina felt like skipping on her way back to the lodge, but the paths were far too icy for that. She needed to get home as soon as possible. She had a good feeling that things were turning out well. She daren't channel her thoughts as to why. There had been far too many disappointments in the past – she didn't want to know her exact fate.

Standing outside Millie's Lakeside Lodge and fumbling around in her pocket, Seraphina realised she'd left home without her keys. She rang the doorbell and waited outside in the cold. Danny was taking his time. She hoped he wasn't in the shower – or, even worse, gone out for the day. Peering through the lounge window, she could see no sign of life.

The sound of crunching footsteps in the snow preceded a tap on her shoulder. Her heart quickened in fear. She became rooted to the spot. 'What do you want?'

'A room for the night would be good.'

Seraphina spun round. 'Justin! What are you still doing here?'

'Just blame it on Prancer and Dancer. Those rocking horses took up two seats each. I could be annoyed that the neighbours gave them priority over me, but who am I to complain? It just means that I get to spend a bit longer in the snow with a beautiful woman.'

'How long are you staying?'

Justin pulled the keys Danny had given him out of his pocket and handed them to Seraphina.

'As long as you want me.'

Seraphina's heart pounded as she unlocked the door to the lodge. If Justin met up to the expectations of her mother and Edna Appleby, then there was an excellent chance he would be staying for quite some time.

*

Back at No. 11 Nasturtium Close, Edna placed the peg doll on her dressing table. She looked out of her bedroom window at No. 18 over the road. The Cassidy's weren't home yet; they no doubt had to make a few stops on the way. She saw the Lacey's car pull onto the drive next door and smiled at the sight of Prancer on the back seat. Bill had brought Dancer in from their car; he was waiting downstairs in the lounge for when the children arrived home.

Edna's heart was full of happiness. The holiday with the neighbours had given her a new lease of life. She was finally one of them. With another little one on the way in the Cassidy household, her Fairy

Godmother skills would continue to be in demand.

Bill was busy downstairs lighting the fire, and Edna had an urge to do something that she'd put off for over sixty-five years. She opened her wardrobe and pulled out a wooden box that belonged to her mother. Edna lifted the lid and gazed into Mystic Marigold Mayweather's crystal ball. She only allowed herself a little glance. It was just enough for her to establish that Sharon Cassidy was pregnant with twins.

Edna replaced the lid and pushed the box to the back of her wardrobe. She closed the door and allowed a feeling of excitement to wash over her; Prancer and Dancer would be getting a lot of use over the next few years. Edna knew that Seraphina would be delighted with that.

Another thought crossed Edna's mind; when Justin and Seraphina got married, Edna would come face-to-face with that horrible man again. Raymondo wouldn't miss his granddaughter's wedding. Edna closed her eyes and was comforted by the thought that she had until summer next year before that happened.

Bill called from downstairs. 'Edna! The children are home. I'll pop over with Dancer. I'll knock for Don, next door. He can take Prancer over at the same time.'

Edna watched the delivery of rocking horses from her bedroom window and vowed never again to have a "bad day". Being able to see into the future had many advantages that she'd overlooked before.

The doorbell rang, and Edna went downstairs to answer it. It was Carol, holding the pregnancy test. 'The bin bag ripped when Don was taking the rubbish out. Someone's pregnant. Please tell me it's not Amy.'

Edna held her shoulders back. Why would Carol be asking her unless the neighbours were embracing her psychic ability? Edna felt quite important. She responded simply, 'It's not Amy.'

Carol let out a sigh of relief. 'Thank goodness. I'll just keep quiet then, and not mention it to Dora.' Carol headed back down the garden path. Edna watched as her next-door-neighbour opened the gate before glancing over her shoulder. 'Thank you so much, Edna. You really made the holiday for everyone. We'll have to do it again sometime.'

Edna blushed and waved. They would definitely be going back to Little Marchampton next year, and Edna could predict when: Saturday, July the 30th was the perfect day for a wedding. She wouldn't tell Carol; it was best not to spoil the surprise.

****

Printed in Great Britain
by Amazon